CURSED TO DIE

Under the reign of Emperor Hadrian (117—138 AD), the power of the Roman Empire reaches to the borders of the known world, and even the most remote provinces enjoy unprecedented peace and prosperity.

On the well-fortified northern border of the empire, the Limes, lies the future world city of Vienna—Vindobona—at this point no more than a legionary base, flanked by two insignificant civilian settlements.

The whims of the gods are unfathomable. The man of antiquity is only a plaything in their power. If he nevertheless dares to take his fate into his own hands, he must use magic. And sometimes in this way he plunges into ruin....

I

"I bring great news, Thanar! There may be a way to save Alma!" Layla announced as she jumped out of her carriage onto the front lawn of my house.

She came running up to me, hugged me warmly in greeting and kissed me on both cheeks, which no longer caused astonished looks between her two companions, a coachman and an armed guard. They were used to the somewhat unusual behavior of the beautiful Nubian by now—Layla came from that mysterious kingdom, deep in the heart of Africa.

Layla had never been much concerned with the question of what manners were appropriate for a woman. The fact that she greeted another man—me—so warmly, even though she was the partner of the camp commander of Vindobona's garrison, was no longer surprising to anyone.

The coachman worked in the legionary camp, but the guard was actually in my service. However, he was so fond of Layla that he almost always accompanied her when she was traveling alone. She trusted him blindly, and I had no objection to putting him at her disposal. His name was Telephus, and he was a former gladiator, legendary for his fearsome axe fighting. He'd had to give up his illustrious arena career, however, because his eyesight had badly deteriorated. He could still see well enough for everyday tasks, such as being Layla's escort, but in gladiatorial combat, where quick reflexes and perfectly honed senses could mean the difference between life and death, his diminished eyesight had become a deadly weakness. That was why he now worked for me, and I had never regretted hiring him.

Marcellus, the aforementioned camp commander and Layla's paramour, never put it directly into words, but it was probably fine by him that none of his legionaries gave Layla an escort. He was aware that her paths were often quite unorthodox, and led to the strangest places. Or that she rarely behaved as one would expect of the mistress of a legate. If he had given her a companion from the camp to guard her along her way, he would inevitably have gossiped about it to his soldier friends, and soon the entire legion would have known about Layla's activities.

Marcellus was a self-confident young nobleman, and although he was not overly conscious of his rank and reputation, he was not necessarily eager to become the laughingstock of the legionary camp—let alone all of Vindobona. He was in the public eye and enjoyed the attention he received. On the other hand, he so adored Layla that he practically ate out of her hand, although he would never have admitted to it publicly. She had the freedom of a king's jester in her dealings with him, and enjoyed it to the fullest.

But what was I actually doing here? I was thinking about Layla's companion, about Marcellus, instead of grasping the words that had just fallen from Layla's lips.

There may be a way to save Alma. Had she really said that? Or was it just the desperation in my soul, hoping against hope to hear good news?

I gave myself a jolt and asked, "What are you saying? Salvation for Alma? Are you serious about that? By what means?" We had already tried everything.

Layla nodded her head, even though the gesture was accompanied by a tentative smile. It was rare for her to appear so uncertain.

"I'll tell you everything, Thanar," she said. "Shall we go into the house—or into the garden?"

It was early May and summer had already arrived in our northern province, which was also unusual. Vindobona is a legionary base on the northern border of the empire, the so-called Limes. So it wasn't exactly what one would have called a place of eternal spring. The sun god generally favored more southern climes.

But this year the divine Sol was well-disposed towards us: the smaller courtyards and the large garden of my estate were already blooming and fragrant, fountains were splashing away peacefully, and bees and butterflies were busy at work, buzzing all around us. It could have been truly idyllic if I weren't trembling every hour for my beloved Alma.

The dark shadow hovering over her—what harm would it do in the end? It seemed to me that she was on the verge of losing her mind, and I blamed myself for her condition. We hadn't been a couple long, but I felt my constant involvement in murder cases had led to Alma's terrible suffering and grief.

Layla and I took our seats on the comfortable couches in one of my leafy courtyards, where we wouldn't be disturbed, and she immediately began to recount a wild story.

"I've heard of a healer," she announced, "who is said to perform true miracles. Dexippa, the baker in the camp suburb, told me about her. You know her—she runs that tiny store where I love to buy the sweet bread."

I nodded, even though I really didn't want to talk about bread right now. Everyone knew of old Dexippa and her heavenly delicacies.

"Keep talking," I demanded restlessly.

Layla complied with my request. "Chelion, Dexippa's son, who was a slave in the house of Latobios, died recently. And Dexippa must have heard that I ... well, that you and I...."

She broke off—and I looked at her in amazement. Layla was not usually at a loss for words. She had never formally studied the art of rhetoric, but she knew how to express herself. Despite her gentle nature, her words could sometimes be the sharpest of daggers.

"Continue," I demanded again. I was eager to learn more about this healer, even though I didn't quite understand what she would have to do with a dead slave. Surely she had not brought him back from the realm of the dead?

"So, what I was going to say," Layla explained herself, "is I guess Dexippa had learned that you and I were acting as *Detectores*. That we solve crimes—specifically, murder cases."

A surprised sound escaped my lips. What Layla had said was correct, of course. After we had found ourselves unintentionally involved in heinous murders several times, and felt cursed by the gods because of it, Layla had taken the bull by the horns—figuratively speaking—although I could easily imagine her doing such a deed quite literally.

Am I exaggerating? Perhaps; I may be accused of having an overly effusive opinion of Layla. Perhaps I should also mention that my heart had really once belonged to her, before I gave it to Alma. But actually that isn't relevant in terms of the report I want to give here.

In any case, Layla had explained to me—as far as our involvement in these most heinous violent crimes was concerned—the following: perhaps it was not a curse that we were under, but rather a gift that the gods had given to us. Perhaps the immortals wanted us to help other people, in solving violent crimes committed against their loved ones, friends, or family members. In the Roman Empire it was everyone's responsibility to bring murderers to justice, and if not everyone was capable of solving crimes, apprehending and prosecuting the perpetrator, then professional homicide investigators were—how shall I put it—let's just say there was a gap in the market. And Layla was determined to fill it.

So we had both made the decision to snoop for other people in the future, and had given ourselves the full-bodied name of Detectores.

So far we had not actively offered our services to anyone, or even advertised them publicly. Legate Marcellus was not very enthusiastic about this latest crazy pursuit of his partner—as one can easily imagine. As I said, he tolerated Layla's unusual behavior to a large extent, but there were limits. And hunting down murderers, or putting herself directly in harm's way, was clearly outside of them.

Apparently our successes in the murder cases we had already solved had nevertheless made their way around Vindobona, and had reached the ears of Dexippa the baker via the usual gossip channels.

I had known the woman for a long time. She actually did

bake the best bread in town, but when you shopped with her you had to be careful that she didn't yak you to death. Her tongue never seemed to be still, and she had a firm opinion on practically everything that happened in our sleepy province.

"Dexippa asked me to investigate the death of her son Chelion," Layla said. "She even offered me a hefty sum for my help—which I declined, of course."

"Of course," I said. After all, we had not intended to offer our skills as detectives for a fee. Layla was more than generously provided for by Marcellus, and I earned a good living as a merchant.

In the meantime, I was quite confused by Layla's explanations. "But what does the baker's dead son have to do with a healer who might be able to help Alma?"

Layla grimaced intensely. "Well, um, this healer—her name is Luscinia—supposedly performed a true miracle in the house of Latobios, the very house where Chelion served as a slave. He was a reader and a scribe, and had been with the family for a very long time."

"Wait," I interrupted her, "The house of *Latobios* you say? Not the famous charioteer...?"

"Luscinia managed to save his favorite horse from certain death. Before that, Latobios had consulted just about every medic, healer, and herbalist in the city, had offered exceedingly generous sacrifices to the gods in the temple, had even tried out some tinctures and cures from shady quacks on the poor steed, but nothing worked. Until Luscinia appeared—a beautiful name, by the way, don't you think?"

I nodded, lost in thought. Luscinia meant something like

nightingale. A pretty name indeed, but I was completely indifferent to that at this point. Bringing a horse back from death's door was one thing....

"And the death of this Chelion that Dexippa asked you to investigate ... what does that have to do with the healing of the horse?" I asked. I had a feeling as if my skull was going to explode soon if Layla kept beating around the bush. A baker, a dead slave, a legendary charioteer, his doomed steed, a miracle healer.... I shook my head involuntarily, struggling to come out of a daze.

Layla cleared her throat and hesitated before continuing. She actually seemed embarrassed, which was not often the case. She was hiding something from me, or I didn't quite understand what she was getting at.

"The thing is, Thanar," she began, "Dexippa is of the firm opinion that while Luscinia may have saved the horse, in doing so she is also responsible for the death of her son."

"Please," I rubbed my forehead, "what do you mean?"

"Luscinia is no ordinary healer, you know."

"Oh?"

II

Again Layla cleared her throat and tugged at the folds of her robe, even though it clung perfectly to her body and there was certainly nothing to improve upon in my view.

Her silky tunic and matching cape were the same color as the sky above: a soft summery blue that set off Layla's beautiful black skin perfectly.

She chewed her lower lip for a moment, seeming to argue with herself. But finally she said, "A witch, Thanar. Luscinia is a witch. She may be an herbalist, but she heals primarily with her own magical powers. And anyone who can protect, or even save lives in this way, is said to be, well—"

Again, she faltered.

"She can also take lives, you want to say," I completed the sentence for her.

She nodded wordlessly.

"And you want me to send Alma to this potential murderer? Are you out of your mind?"

Layla passed over my remark. "Well, Dexippa at any rate is of the firm opinion that Luscinia is responsible for Chelion's death," she said instead. "His body was found entirely intact, you know, without any visible wounds. And even the very morning of the day of his death he was in the best of health. Chelion was a strong man in the prime of life, as they say: in good health and as strong as an ox. At least that is how Dexippa described him to me. When I arrived at the house of

Latobios a few days later to see the body for myself, it had long since been taken away, but the slaves in the house confirmed to me what Dexippa had claimed. No wounds, no illness, no outward signs of a struggle. Chelion had simply been found dead in a corridor, as if he had been struck down there by the hand of the gods."

Layla fell silent for a moment, then added, "I hope you won't think I'm crazy, but the house of Latobios—as magnificent as the estate may be—really does seem to have a dark shadow hanging over it. I felt it quite clearly when I visited there. Something is not right about the place. One could truly think that something evil has taken root within the walls, although of course I can't tell if it has taken up residence there because of Luscinia."

This was another unusual remark for Layla. Normally she was more rational than any man, and certainly not a timid little mouse who thought she perceived dark omens around every corner—or looming over the estates of charioteers. She always approached any seemingly intractable problem with her mind first, and that was as sharp as a deadly blade.

On the other hand, the magic of witches was really not to be trifled with.

"Hmmm," I replied after pondering intensely for a brief while. "If Luscinia saved the life of this doomed horse by means of a dark spell, she may have brought ruin upon Latobios and his *familia*, all his employees, and even his slaves. Is it not said that people saved or even revived by demonic spells are cursed forever? That they are in league with—or rather in debt to—dark forces, because they called to their aid corrupted gods or spirits who gave them a new life force? And often, such spells only become possible in the first place due to the shedding of innocent blood. I'm sure I don't have to tell you that."

Sorcerers who summoned spirits and forced them to be at their service often procured these undead helpers themselves without scruple—by summarily murdering the suitable man, or even a suitable woman. Those who were fearless, brutal, and dangerous in life generally also tend to be such a spirit after their demise. And as for the undead helpers, the same was probably also true: the more homicidal they were, the better.

The profession of witch or sorcerer was not for the squeamish, even if many of these accusations were only superstitious gossip.

"This is exactly what Dexippa thinks," Layla exclaimed, "that her son had to die because the horse was allowed to live! But that's madness, isn't it? You don't believe in such nonsense, do you?"

"Of course not," I said quickly—but perhaps not with the necessary emphasis.

Layla gave me an inquiring look. "What do you really think about it, Thanar? Tell me the truth! Do you think it's possible that Dexippa could be right?"

I hunched my shoulders and tried to explain myself to her. "Well, let's put it this way: after all we've seen in the meantime, in terms of death and ruin, I truly can no longer rule anything out. Evil is omnipresent, whether by the hand of man or the hidden will of the gods ... or the dark magic of a witch. Who is truly able to fathom all of life's secrets? And who would dare to claim that witches and wizards are all just charlatans, who in truth cannot do anything? Cunning deceivers, who only captivate the people with clever gossip and pretended magic? I am sure that this may be true for the majority, but one or two wizards may have powers of which we can't conceive. And the way you describe this Luscinia...."

"She is said to have already accomplished many great things!" Layla interrupted me. She nodded several times in rapid succession, as if she could thereby convince herself of her own words.

On the one hand she was visibly uncomfortable with the whole story she was telling me, but on the other she seemed to have already taken a fancy to this alleged witch. In her words admiration resonated, and there was a special sparkle in her dark eyes when she said Luscinia's name.

Layla had a weakness for extraordinary women, let's just say. In the past she had befriended many: druids who were feared and persecuted by the Romans as being the worst kind of demons; a gladiatrix who was said to be a man-killer; or innocent girls who later turned out to be deadly Furies. So why not now a witch who possessed power over life and death itself? And one who had even possibly sacrificed the life of a slave for that of a very expensive horse.

When it came to Layla's murderous friends, whatever would be next? I could see myself following her into the depths of the Underworld ... but no, even if she wanted to befriend Proserpina herself—the wife of Pluto, Lord of the Underworld—it was no longer up to me to save her from such folly and suicidal adventures. That was Marcellus's task now. *He* was her lover. I had to see to it that Alma did not soon disappear into that same world of shadows, if we did not finally find relief for her suffering.

Layla snapped me out of my thoughts. "I was making inquiries about Luscinia," she said, "very discreetly, of course."

"You have done well in that," I replied, "but at the same time, I hope you are aware of how dangerous it could be for you if you make closer acquaintance with this woman. For if Marcellus were to learn that you are interested in the witches' dark arts, perhaps even wishing to consult such a magician yourself—well, he would tear your head off, I fear. Both of us, in fact, if we sought out this sorceress together."

"I'm well aware of that," Layla confirmed with a serious expression, "but what I wanted to add is, in my research I learned truly miraculous things about Luscinia. She is said to be able to effect a cure even when the best *medicus* has reached the end of his wisdom. Before she came here to Vindobona, she is said to have worked in the East—in Aquincum, they say, where she saved more than one person from certain death. From newborn infants even to elderly men."

Aquincum was a legionary city on the Danubius River Limes, just like Vindobona. It lay six or seven days' journey east of us, and I had already visited it on my travels as a merchant. In the past, before I could delegate the most arduous journeys to my servants, I had myself very often traveled the many roads of the Empire and beyond. For I trade in those luxury goods which the Romans covet—and also in those which they themselves produce. For the latter, there is great demand among the peoples north of the border, the Germanic tribes to which I myself belong, even though I have now lived in Vindobona for a long time and have devoted myself entirely to the Roman way of life. In any case, there is hardly a corner of the empire that I have not been to.

"And what do you hear from Aquincum, about your witch?" I asked Layla.

She furrowed her brow. "Contradictory information, just like here in Vindobona, even though she has only been with us for a short time. There is talk of numerous miraculous cures, but also of vile curses and damaging spells of which she is said to be capable. Disease and death are allegedly her constant companions. It is even rumored that the black dog of the goddess Hekate has been seen walking the streets of Aquincum at night."

"Well, wonderful," I said. "That truly sounds promising!"

Hekate was the dark mistress of magic and necromancy. She was worshiped at crossroads and watched over the gates between the world of the living and the dead. In the animal kingdom, she commanded dogs, lizards, toads, and owls, and she kept a black dog as a pet, so to speak. He may not have three heads like the more famous Cerberus, but it was said that his look alone could drive a man mad or even kill him. Whoever was struck by his foul breath would do well to make up his will as soon as possible.

"Marcellus will have this Luscinia crucified without hesitation when he finds out about her," I said to Layla. "I hope you realize that."

Dark magic, damaging spells, curses, deadly potions and the like were punishable by death in the Roman Empire. Without any ifs, ands, or buts. Many of the neighboring peoples did the same. Whoever harmed a person had to pay for their act—regardless of whether he used an ax or the evil eye for his purpose. It made no difference in the sight of the law.

"Marcellus will be out for a few more days," Layla told me impassively, "weeks, possibly. He's inspecting the auxiliary camps to the west: Cannabiaca, Asturis, and Augustianis. Before he returns, I want to have cleared up Chelion's death. And we should talk to Alma, I think, and let her decide for herself if she wants to try her luck with the witch's healing spells. I'd imagine she'd be willing to do almost anything by now, just to finally find some relief."

I nodded wordlessly; Layla was right, of course. And I myself would have done anything to help my beloved Alma. I hated watching so helplessly while she wasted away.

"So, when did Dexippa give you this assignment?" I asked. "To find out about the death of her son. When did this Chelion die?"

"It has been just under a week since she approached me, and two weeks since he passed away."

"But why didn't you tell me sooner?" I asked. "Weren't we going to be detectives together? Are you so tired of living that you would want to risk approaching a murderer alone?"

Layla bowed her head. She knew that my rebuke was based only on my concern for her—and that I was right about her recklessness. She was a smart woman, with a real talent for solving crime and murder, but that didn't make her invincible or even immortal. She tended at times to take far too great a risk without thinking about it for even a moment, and she knew that very well.

"You were so worried about Alma," she said, "so busy seeing doctors, making offerings at the temple, keeping vigil at her bedside, sacrificing your own sleep ... so I didn't want to involve you in this murder, or indeed the whole witch business. If it even was a murder at all. I'm far from convinced of it."

What could I say to that?

"We'll help the baker together, okay?" I said finally after we'd stared at each other silently for a while. "That is, we will at least try. If we can solve the case before Marcellus returns; otherwise we'll have to give up on it, because he'd have me quartered if he found out I was aiding you in your snooping. But I think you know that. And we'll ask Alma if we should arrange a meeting with that witch for her own sake. Where is this Luscinia to be found? Surely she hasn't just moved into a house in town?"

Witches were—because of their forbidden arts—outcasts who lived on the fringes of society. They hid in dark forests, in caves, in abandoned houses or homesteads that no one visited anymore, often because they were said to be haunted. Witches did not shun ghosts or the undead; on the contrary, they were at home in their world.

"She's supposed to have set up camp in the woods south of the civilian town," Layla said. "There's a helper who serves as a contact. Her name is Sagana, and she has rented a room at an inn on the Limes Road. It's in Rufius's roadhouse, to the east of the civilian town, you certainly know it."

I nodded. Among the local population, the hostel bore the derisive name of *Rufius's Rat Hole*. And not without good reason, I had found. The owner was a nasty cutthroat who charged unsuspecting travelers exorbitant prices for his run-down rooms, bug-filled beds and barely edible foods.

"Only shady riffraff descend to that place," I told Layla, "and the poorest travelers who can't afford to shun vermin."

The corners of Layla's mouth quirked. "That's true. But such places are the only accommodation for travelers who have no wealthy local business partners with whom they could find quarters. Or for those people who don't want to be seen or heard by the respectable citizens of the city. If you don't want to go to Rufius's place, we can also look for Luscinia's helpmate, this Sagana, in the city. She is out and about in the markets, in the Forum, and in the Thermae, where she follows the people's gossip. She finds people who may be unhappy in love—or lonely, bitter, and out for revenge—and she also hangs around the temples, where she approaches those who offer the most expensive sacrifices to the gods, because their longings, hopes or fears are the greatest. She offers the services of Luscinia to all of these people, and presumably finds plenty of customers willing to pay."

"I guess we fit into that group perfectly," I grumbled.

Layla passed over my comment. "And one more thing, Thanar," she said instead, "we have a brave volunteer who wants to try out the witch's *healing* skills before we lead Alma to her—should she even choose to consult Luscinia."

"A volunteer?" I asked incredulously. What had Layla cooked up now?

"It's Telephus," she said, "and the suggestion really came from him; I certainly didn't push him into it. He accompanies me so often on my walks that he naturally witnessed my inquiries about Luscinia. And he wants to be the first to be treated by the witch—for his failing eyesight, you see. He's hoping to be able to stop the deterioration of his eyesight with the help of Luscinia's powerful magic. He's a very brave man, but he's afraid of sinking into eternal darkness, even in the prime of his life."

I sighed. I had come to regard Telephus as a friend and would have liked to stop him from taking such a risk. But I also knew how desperate he was, even though he might appear stoically calm on the outside. He had already tried everything possible to save his eyesight, but without any success worth mentioning so far.

"Let's see how Alma is doing right now," I suggested to Layla. "Whether she's responsive."

"How is she feeling today?" Layla wanted to know. There was deep concern in her tone.

"No worse than yesterday," I replied in frustration. "Nemesis is with her; she promised me she would keep watch by her bedside if Alma could get some sleep. You see, she now tries to close her eyes for a few hours during the day. At night, she daren't anymore."

Nemesis was the gladiatrix I mentioned earlier. She had been an accused man-killer—wrongly, as it had turned out in the end.

Since those murders—which I reported in my last chronicle—she'd been a guest in my house, together with Optimus, a veteran of the Legion, whom I also called a friend. The two had become close, loving each other in a somewhat shy way, like two people who had lived alone for a long time and had to get used to having a companion by their side again.

Nemesis had made friends with Alma—the two were almost like siblings—and Layla was the third in their sisterhood. An inseparable trio that was unparalleled. I could boast that the most unusual women in our province had found each other under my roof.

III

Alma was on fire when we told her about the witch. It almost seemed to me that with Layla's suggestion, and her glowing descriptions of Luscinia's healing miracles, a little strength returned to Alma's tired limbs. It was a sight that gladdened my heart.

Alma needed to assure herself several times, with many awkward questions, that Telephus was not sacrificing himself for her sake as a witchcraft test subject. But when we had convinced her that this was not the case, she burned to see Luscinia. The thought of consulting a witch seemed, to my surprise, hardly to frighten her at all. On the contrary, it seemed to fill her with new hope that her fate was not yet sealed after all.

We agreed that Telephus, Layla and I would first go and see Sagana, the assistant, who had stayed at Rufius's Rat Hole—pardon me—Rufius's *Rest House*. After that, we were going to get a close personal look at the witch before taking the risk of leading Alma to her.

My beloved was by now so exhausted that even the short journey to that patch of woods where Luscinia had supposedly set up camp would cause her a great deal of strain. However, she was determined to make the journey after we had made our appeal to the witch.

So, barely half an hour later, Telephus, Layla, and I were already in my fastest wagon, hitched to my finest horses, heading for Rufius's inn.

The journey led us first over the Danubius Bridge and into the suburb of the legionary camp, then further on into the civilian city of Vindobona, which lay southeast of it, and then finally into that flophouse of Rufius's, whose most tempting comforts I have already described to my luxury-inclined readers. Rufius's rest house was located directly on the Limes Road that led from Vindobona to our provincial capital, Carnuntum.

We were on the road for about an hour and I used the time to ask Layla about the dead slave, Chelion. I wanted to know everything she had found out about him so far, including his early demise.

As morbid as it probably sounds, this maybe-murder case that Layla was trying to solve on behalf of our local chatty master baker was a welcome distraction for me.

If it was in my power I would gladly help to ease Dexippa's grief over her deceased son a little, by getting her the answers she was yearning for. Anything would be better than spending my time in endless musings over Alma's terrible suffering and my own part in it. Such depressing thoughts did not help her either, as she perceived my worry too. It was therefore better for the both of us if I remained busy. So if Chelion had indeed been murdered, I would not rest until the culprit paid the extreme penalty for it, hanging on the cross.

"Unfortunately, I've been able to find out very little so far," Layla confessed. "I first had to gain access to the house of Latobios. I couldn't just show up there unannounced and ask to be let in. That would have been highly improper and more than a little suspicious."

"Since when do you care about good manners, my dear?" I teased Layla.

A grin flitted across her face, but she continued, "So I made an attempt to invite myself into the house via its mistress, so to speak, and I succeeded. I had already met Hersilia, the wife of Latobios, a time or two in Vindobona, but we had barely exchanged a few words. Now I sent her a messenger, asking to be allowed to visit her. I pretended that I admired her wardrobe *to the utmost*, and posthaste sent to ask if she could not recommend her cloth merchant to me." She smirked.

"A most clever thread of enquiry," I commented. And then suddenly had to laugh. I, an old fool, was a little proud of the pun I had managed to make, albeit unintentionally. Wardrobe—fabric dealer—*thread.* Quite clever, I thought. You may forgive me this touch of childish pride. It did me good to be able to laugh freely for once, after days and even weeks filled with sorrow.

My linguistic entendre seemed to pass Layla by unnoticed. She didn't comment on it with a single syllable, she didn't even manage a smile.

Visibly focused fully on her new case, she continued, "Well, I didn't have to resort to lying. Hersilia is indeed a very well-dressed woman. Whenever I've met her, she has been wearing the most expensive fabrics, in the most splendid colors. Even fine silks from faraway Asia, in which she looked like a queen. She is a beautiful woman, after all. Have you ever met her yourself, Thanar?"

"Possibly; I can't remember. I don't know Latobios well, let alone his spouse."

As far as great beauties were concerned, I had only ever had eyes for Layla—and now for Alma. Even though they were as different as water is from fire—the blond, fair-skinned German from the far north, and the mysterious dark sphinx from the Nubian deserts—I found them equally irresistible.

"So how did your meeting with Hersilia go?" I picked up the *thread* of conversation again. "How did you go from fashion and clothing to talking about the death of the slave Chelion?"

"It wasn't as difficult as you might think. As I said, there seemed to me to be an ominous dark cloud hovering over the entire estate, and Hersilia also seemed as if—oh, I don't know how to describe it—as if she herself were walking through the realm of the dead?"

"What's that supposed to mean, exactly?" I objected.

"It's really hard to put into words. In itself, Hersilia is not only a very fashionable and attractive lady, but one of the most graceful women I've ever met. She is fair-skinned and blonde like Alma, with a complexion like the finest alabaster. Though she is approaching forty, she does not look a day over twenty-five. She may be consummate in the art of makeup, but that is certainly not all. Her grace extends far beyond that."

"So she's beautiful, lovely, a real feast for the eyes—" I interjected a little impatiently. "I've got that now, I think. So then what?"

"Right, yes, but the point is: when I spoke to her the day before yesterday, she was only a shadow of her former self. She had barely dressed up, and looked pale and exhausted. There was no hint of gracefulness. So I came to speak quite directly about the dead slave, and inquired whether his death had perhaps ... well, let's say, 'frightened' the household. I had overheard the slaves and servants in the house, in fact, whispering—similar to Dexippa before—of the dark imprecations of the witch who had recently saved the master's horse from death. I did not directly indicate to Hersilia that I thought she herself was also afflicted with this fear, but that was not necessary. She admitted of her own accord and quite freely that Chelion's death had affected her deeply. '*When such a happy and healthy person in your immediate vicinity is so suddenly snatched from life, one inevitably fears how long one's own life span may last...*' were the words from her own mouth."

I nodded; I could well understand her feelings. Who would willingly look death in its gloomy face? Even more so if it was an inexplicable, perhaps even violent death, behind which one believed the forces of evil to be at work. When those are the forces at play, anyone could feel vulnerable.

"I then decided to be upfront about my mission," Layla went on. "I told Hersilia that Chelion's mother didn't want to believe her son had died of natural causes, and that she had asked me to do some investigating."

"I suppose that might have astonished Hersilia, wouldn't it?" I said. "That you, the legate's companion, should act as a professional snoop for a mere baker."

"It's possible," Layla replied, "but if I astonished her with my words, it was hardly noticeable. She seemed, as I said, powerless and completely exhausted, as if all vitality had left her. Well, in any case, she readily gave me permission to look around her house, to talk to the slaves and servants.... She assured me that she, too, wanted Chelion's death to be solved. She seemed to have been quite sympathetic toward him while he was alive. She told me that he had often read to her from her favorite novels, and from the writings of the great philosophers, and he had composed long letters for her when she wanted to correspond with friends."

We were just passing through one of the better quarters of the civilian town on our way, and my gaze wandered over the quite handsome mansions that were lined up here on both sides of the street. Soon we would reach the eastern gate of the city, and then it was not far to the inn of Rufius.

"One thing I don't understand," I said to Layla. "Dexippa, our baker, the dead man's mother—she was once a slave herself, so it may not surprise anyone that her son was also a captive. But she was able to buy herself free from her master a long time ago and has been running this bakery ever since, hasn't she? I must have known her store for almost ten years, and it seems to be doing very well. How come Dexippa didn't buy her son out long ago? It seems to me that she was exceedingly fond of him, wasn't she?"

"I wondered about that too, Thanar, and so I asked her about it. She answered me that Latobios, her son's master, had not allowed him to ransom himself."

"Really? How unusual! Was his reader and scribe so indispensable to him?"

"We should ask him that as soon as we get the chance," Layla said with a frown.

IV

Rufius's inn must have been recently renovated, because, at least from the outside, it looked a little bit more inviting than the Rat House I remembered.

Not that I had ever stayed here myself, but in my early years as a merchant, when I had still traded in goods from what could sometimes be called dubious sources, I had met here once or twice with a business partner to discuss a purchase or sale. As I've said, out-of-town hostels for travelers were ideal for discreet dealings. You could almost say that I had laid the foundation of my fortune in places like Rufius's roadhouse. Not a very nice thought, but that was the way it was back then.

Fortunately, those times were now behind me. Since Marcellus, the legate of Vindobona, had become my friend, I conducted my business in the most exemplary manner. Most importantly, I felt no urge to feel the sand of the arena under the soles of my feet and be food for the beasts there.

A large sign to the right of the entrance gate of Rufius's roadhouse advertised various amenities: there was talk of hot meals, "excellent" wines, and "tender" company for lonely travelers. In addition, the guests' horses found space in their own stable building, where the conveyances they pulled could also be repaired if necessary.

On the forecourt and also inside the house, as far as one could see from the outside, there was lively activity. Slaves and servants ran around as if badly startled, and behind the open gate of the stable building the most diverse collection of wagons and carts were crowded. The neighing of horses somewhere beyond reached my ears. Apparently Rufius's rest house was better frequented than I recalled.

The landlady—Rufius's wife—came hurrying up as we climbed out of the cart. Her rear end was so wide that she waddled toward us like a duck—and her put-on friendliness immediately fell away when we let her know that we weren't going to take one of her rooms.

I gave our coachman money for a few cups to slake his thirst in the inn's tavern while we inquired about Sagana's lodgings.

The landlady knew immediately who we were talking about. Apparently we were not the first to ask about the witch's assistant that day. She directed us to the second floor, which we found via a narrow, worm-eaten staircase.

The wood groaned under our footsteps as if the staircase might collapse at any moment. The renovation of the house, I thus understood, had definitely been limited to the most necessary work on the outer facade only. And that was probably enough; once a weary traveler got off his horse or climbed out of his wagon and entered the inn in anticipation of a soft bed, he could hardly bring himself to turn around and return to the dusty country road—knowing full well that the next inn might be several hours away and might not offer any better comfort.

We had hardly reached the top of the stairs when Telephus suddenly raised his hand and jerked to a halt. Since he was walking in front of us—which he usually did, always trying to protect us from every conceivable danger—I almost ran into him. Layla, who had been the last to climb the steep stairs, crashed into my back.

"What's going on?" I asked quietly, turning to the former gladiator in alarm.

Telephus wordlessly raised his hand and pointed to the door of what we knew to be Sagana's chamber.

"Can't you hear it?" he whispered to us. "Someone is with her."

I hadn't heard a thing, and Layla also shook her head. Telephus might have eye problems, but the ex-gladiator's hearing still seemed as excellent as ever.

The next moment his suspicions that Sagana had a visitor were confirmed, for suddenly we heard a man's voice coming from the chamber in question.

The door of the chamber seemed to be made of surprisingly high-quality wood, which muffled all sounds that ordinarily penetrated from the room to the outside. But whoever was a guest of the witch's handmaid was suddenly seized by a blazing anger, and he began to roar.

"She must suffer the most hideous pain, do you hear!" thundered the muffled voice from beyond, which definitely belonged to a man.

The answer came much quieter, barely intelligible, even though I had unceremoniously rushed to the door of the chamber and shamelessly pressed my ear against the wood.

The second, quieter voice belonged to a woman. Sagana, most probably. "So tame yourself then, man, or shall you be heard throughout the house?" she huffed.

Immediately afterwards, she was a little more conciliatory. Her tone became audibly friendlier. "Don't worry," she implored her visitor. "It will happen as you wish. *Very soon.*"

The next moment, the door of the chamber flew open.

I could just manage to jump aside to avoid being caught in the act of flagrant eavesdropping. A big beefy guy stormed out of the room and almost ran me over.

For a moment the man looked startled, frozen into a pillar of salt, and glared at me. He probably felt caught out. But in the next moment he was again master of his senses.

He nodded at me, a quick and not particularly friendly greeting, then pushed past me and my companions and hurried down the stairs. It had all happened so quickly that the next moment I wondered if I had really heard those vile words filled with fiery hatred, or whether my ears had been playing tricks on me.

"A legionary *optio*," Layla whispered to us as the man disappeared and his footsteps faded down the corridor. She seemed to have recognized the rake. "I don't remember his name," she explained, "but I've encountered him a time or two in the legionary camp."

"His name is Gorgonius, if I remember correctly," Telephus interposed. "I too have met him ... in one tavern or another. An unpleasant fellow, I can tell you that."

"I've heard as much. I wonder who she may be, the one who is to suffer such hideous pain?" I mused to myself in a whisper. "A beloved one who spurned him? An unfaithful mistress?"

The soldiers of the Roman legions were not officially allowed to marry, but this did not prevent them—especially in distant provinces like ours—from keeping a mistress in the camp suburb, or even starting their own family there.

I received no answer to my questions from my two companions, only uncertain looks.

"What do you two think—are we really in the right place, with this dark summoner? One who is ready to cast such evil spells?" I said, speaking aloud the doubts that had risen in me.

Hadn't Layla assured me that Sagana's mistress devoted herself exclusively to well-meaning and healing magic? The words of this Gorgonius had certainly not sounded anything like that.

Telephus jerked to attention and strode courageously toward the door that had slammed shut behind the optio.

"It's well known that witches are paid mostly for damaging spells," he said as he glanced over his shoulder at me. "I won't be discouraged by that. Let's see what this sorceress can do for my eyesight—as long as I don't have to bathe in the blood of newborns to do it, or something similarly unspeakable. I don't think the witch will do anything to *us*. After all, we are paying customers, aren't we?"

Thus determined, Telephus knocked on the door.

The woman who opened to us within a few moments was petite, dark-haired, and wrapped in a colorful robe that gave her quite an elegant appearance. Her eyes were set close together, and were ringed with thick black eyelashes. With exquisite politeness and in excellent Latin, she asked us to enter.

Not the typical servant of a quack or charlatan, it flashed through my mind.

I had found new hope already—which grew increasingly as we took our seats on the modest stools of the chamber, and

Telephus began to tell Sagana his problem.

He modestly concealed his glorious past as a victorious and highly-skilled gladiator. He merely spoke of how he had had to give up earning a living because of his failing eyesight, and that he feared he would be walking with a blind man's cane in just a few years if the deterioration could not be stopped. He asked for an appointment with Luscinia so that he could hear her advice, and hopefully obtain healing thanks to her magical powers.

Sagana listened attentively while I looked around the room. I don't know what I had expected, but to my relief I noticed that there was no cauldron hanging over the hearth, bubbling menacingly and spreading foul fumes. Neither were there dried bats, skinned beasts, or other creatures that witches like to process into powders and potions, hanging to dry from the ceiling beams. I was probably naive, prejudiced, but I had never before actually used the services of a witch.

For the time being, we did not mention a word about Alma and her psychological torment to Sagana. Her master Luscinia should first prove to us on Telephus what she was actually capable of before I risked bringing my poor suffering lover to her.

Sagana proved to be an extremely businesslike woman. She asked Telephus specific questions, which she phrased concisely. Probably she wanted to emphasize that she was a very busy person, and her time was therefore precious—which in turn suggested that her mistress's services must be in great demand.

After Telephus had answered all her questions, she named a sum that brought tears to my eyes. Thirty sesterces she demanded just for bringing Telephus to her master. That was the equivalent of two weeks' wages for a legionary in our province! Not exactly a price that the simple man on the street could readily afford.

It had probably been a mistake for Layla and me to accompany Telephus to the witch's assistant. Sagana had taken one look at Layla's magnificent sky-blue robes, her shoes embroidered by a master's hand, and her golden earrings, and had surely concluded that we were wealthy customers, used to paying for luxuries, who could easily be charged many times the usual fee.

That Telephus would actually be cured of his eye condition was far from guaranteed even with this outrageous sum, and there was the chance Luscinia herself would undoubtedly make further, even higher demands for more money.

"But don't worry," Sagana said in a buoyant tone of conviction to our valiant ex-gladiator, "Luscinia will be able to help you; she is a master of her craft. Your money is well spent."

She instructed us to come back here to the inn in the afternoon of the following day, and promised to lead us to Luscinia's camp and introduce us personally to the sorceress.

When we had climbed back into our wagon in front of the rest house's stables, Layla said, "Let's go to the house of Latobios, shall we? Perhaps the master of the house is available today, and we can ask him about his experience with Luscinia. After all, she is said to have worked a miracle of healing on his horse."

"And shall we take this opportunity to make further inquiries concerning the death of his slave, Chelion?" I added with a twinkle in my eye.

Layla gave me one of her sphinxlike expressions, which could mean anything imaginable. But I couldn't help noticing that a guilty smile flitted across her lips.

I knew Layla. I knew she was determined to solve this suspicious death, as she had promised Dexippa the baker. Sniffing out murderers was her absolute favorite pastime, even if I didn't really believe that anyone had murdered the poor reader. Who would honestly want to kill an insignificant slave in a sleepy corner of the empire?

However, to my shame, I must confess that I was looking forward to working on this case almost as much as Layla apparently was, even if Chelion's death turned out to be nothing more than a tragic accident or simply the premature end of a human life as willed by the gods.

As I said, I of course wanted to help Dexippa gain certainty about her son's fate, but I longed just as much for a distraction from Alma's terrible suffering, which I could only watch helplessly as it grew worse.

On the other hand, I would have loved to be with Alma at every hour of the day and night, to comfort her as best I could, to cheer her up, to pour invigorating soups for her to drink....

But I knew that for my sake she always tried to play down her sufferings on these occasions. When I was with her, she always tried to appear cheerful and strong, instead of admitting to me how she was really feeling. She did this out of love for me, in order that I would not be saddened. However, this bit of theater cost her an incredible amount of strength, which she did not have in her present condition.

And so with a heavy heart I had managed to force myself to only briefly check on her every now and then over the past few days, otherwise leaving her in the care of Layla or of Nemesis the gladiatrix. In front of her closest friends she didn't feel compelled to pretend that everything was fine.

V

The estate of Latobios, a pompous country villa in the Roman style, was located a ways outside the civilian town, but still close to the Limes road. One could see from the size of the building, the surrounding gardens, and the fields and horse pastures that this man had more money than he could ever spend in this lifetime.

Latobios was about my age—in his early forties—which is almost a miracle for a charioteer. In Rome and in those larger cities of the empire that could boast their own circuses, chariot racing was one of the people's favorite amusements.

A daredevil who knew how to steer two-, four- or sometimes even six-horse chariots through the tight curves of the racetrack without breaking his neck, was as great a hero to the public as the most famous gladiators. And his life expectancy was just as short as that of the arena swordsmen or spearmen, even if he did not try to stand up to his competitors by sheer force of arms.

Accidents were the order of the day in the circus; indeed, in some ways the public craved these dramatic spectacles all the greater, the more violent they became, and it was not always only the horses at the end of a race whose bruised or broken bodies had to be picked up from the sands of the arena.

The prize money that a daredevil charioteer could collect was accordingly attractive.

Latobios had originally been born in Vindobona, of mixed

Celtic-Roman blood, and then had an unprecedented career on the racetracks of the Empire, which in the end had led him to Rome. He'd raced in the legendary Circus Maximus, where the most famous races in the world had been held since time immemorial.

In the Eternal City, Latobios had driven for some of the most famous racing teams for years, or rather for decades—first for the Reds and then the Blues, as far as I had heard. As I've said, I have not been closely acquainted with the man and thus have to rely on hearsay. In any case, his countless victories at the Circus Maximus had earned him a fortune that would have made many a high born senatorial family green with envy.

It was rumored that Latobios was worth several million sesterces, and looking at the estate he had built for himself after his return to Vindobona, one could well believe it.

It had been barely a year since this famous son of the city had returned home. He was popular with the people, celebrated and revered, but also envied for his fabulous wealth.

The secret to Latobios's success was his very special relationship with horses. He never tired of telling this to his admirers—and to all the other inhabitants of the city—so that by now all of Vindobona knew about it. Even a barbarian from the northern bank of the Danubius like me had heard it.

The animals seemed to idolize him, and competed to fulfil his every wish. Therefore he had always selected his own horses for the racing teams for which he had competed; indeed, towards the end of his career, he had even had the means to breed the noble steeds for the competition himself.

When he'd finally retired—and returned to his long-lost home of Vindobona—he had accordingly arrived with a large herd of his noble four-legged friends, and it was said that these horses were still his greatest treasure, a feast for the eyes and his greatest passion.

On the estate forecourt there was already a crowd of servants waiting for us, and perfectly manicured flowerbeds and shrubbery adorned the square, which was surrounded by shady columned arcades.

Telephus and the coachman stayed by our wagon and indulged in a chat with these servants of the house, or rather with some of the grooms.

Layla and I indicated that we wished to speak to Hersilia. Layla already knew the lady of the house, and we assumed that we would be allowed to see her without any difficulty, and then be introduced to her husband.

But our plans were thwarted, because in the atrium of the house we were met by Latobios himself—or rather, we were intercepted by him.

He returned our greeting, but then immediately gave Layla a blatantly hostile look.

"What do you want from my wife now?" he exclaimed. "After your last visit, she was utterly distraught! You made her feel quite foolish, with all your talk about our dead slave, and that ridiculous spiel about dark witchcraft spells hanging over the estate and other similar nonsense!" He waved his muscular arms impetuously, as if he were trying to give additional vent to his anger in this way. His words and tone were brutal enough.

Layla indicated a bow with consummate courtesy and

pretended to be contrite. "That was certainly not my intention, Latobios," she said in a voice as sweet as honeyed wine. "I assure you of that. But frankly, your wife made a rather disturbed impression when I first came to her. It seemed to me she was very much afraid of this witch you consulted. And she may believe that the death of your slave may be ... well, related to Luscinia's magic powers. Thanar and I,"—she gave me a sidelong glance—"wanted to talk to you about this very sorceress. We hoped you could recommend her to us, or if necessary, warn us about her. For my best friend, and Thanar's dear companion, needs Luscinia's help; her situation seems utterly hopeless otherwise, and we don't know what else to do—"

She did not get any further. Latobios cut her off with a rude wave of his hand, wrinkling his nose as if he had smelled something rotten.

I felt anger boiling up inside me. No one had the right to treat Layla in this way—even if the charioteer's boorish behavior and attitude may have been the result of a justified concern for his wife.

But before I could intervene, the master of the house had already taken the floor. "If you only care about the well-being of your girlfriend, as you say, then why your interest in the death of my slave?" He hurled the words at Layla. "What do you care about him? Or me? I can afford a hundred more in his place!"

"I have no doubt about that," Layla said in a tone that continued to be very friendly. The charioteer's uncouth demeanor seemed to have impressed her only slightly.

"But Chelion must have been one of your favorite slaves,

wasn't he?" she continued unapologetically. "An excellent scribe and reader?"

Latobios was visibly not in the mood for this conversation, but did finally give her an answer. He probably knew that Layla was the legate of Vindobona's mistress, and that he could not afford—no matter how rich he might be—to simply throw her out of his house. Even more so in the presence of a witness such as yours truly.

"Favorite slave?" he grumbled, then added ill-temperedly, "Where did you get that idea? I rarely used his services. He drew up the odd business document for me, but that was about all. A great letter writer I am not, and I leave the reading to my wife."

He paused for a moment and tightened his impressive shoulders.

Speaking of shoulders, perhaps I should describe the rest of his appearance while I'm at it: he was not what you would call a beau, but still an attractive man. His auburn hair was already a bit sparse, especially on his forehead, but his body still looked like that of a celebrated athlete. I could well imagine that the female fans of the Circus had flocked to his feet.

A touch more politely, he continued, "Chelion was in my service for a very long time. And he was quite capable, I won't deny that. But that doesn't make him irreplaceable. People die, often many years before they reach old age. That's just the way of the world."

Layla nodded, forced a smile, and said, "I heard you didn't grant Chelion the opportunity to buy his freedom. That's why I assumed he was indispensable to you, and—"

Once again Latobios did not let her finish speaking.

"What nonsense," he cried heatedly. "I certainly didn't deny him his freedom! Every one of my slaves can buy his way out as soon as he has saved up enough. I don't want to make a loss, of course, but I don't charge anyone more than the usual sum—after all, I am not an inhuman. As I said, I can buy a hundred new slaves whenever I want."

What an arrogant snob, the thought went through my mind.

Latobios might have a knack for horses, but he was apparently untrained when it came to dealing with people. And did he really have to constantly emphasize what he could afford? His wealth was obvious, even when you lowered your gaze to the tips of your shoes in this house. The floor mosaic, which filled the entirety of the enormous atrium, was so magnificent and so intricately worked that one could have imagined oneself in a senatorial palace. It showed—how could it be otherwise—scenes from the Circus Maximus in Rome. Magnificent horses, sleek racing cars, cheering crowds....

I averted my eyes, but it didn't help. The walls of the room were adorned with equally precious murals, and the open spaces were filled with countless statues and sculptures. If my eyes did not deceive me, most of them were Greek originals, centuries old, and created in the most famous workshops of their time.

A life-size bronze sculpture of a rearing stallion with gleaming jewels for eyes occupied the space behind the water basin that graced the center of the atrium. Latobios was undoubtedly a true horse lover.

Pecunia non olet, money doesn't smell, the Emperor Vespasian had once claimed. But in the house of the former charioteer turned multimillionaire, one had the impression that one was in danger of suffocating amid all the lavish splendor, as if a sickening stench emanated from all the silver, gold and marble that surrounded one in here.

Layla hardly wasted a glance on the treasures the master of the house was displaying in his atrium. She persisted in her questions, acting as friendly and congenial as though she were talking to a very special friend. You really had to admire her for her composure—and her determination at the same time.

"Do you think then that Chelion died of natural causes?" she asked Latobios straightforwardly.

As a result, his features darkened even further.

"What else?" he blurted out.

VI

I decided to come to Layla's rescue. We couldn't risk the former charioteer throwing us out of his house, after all. We had to gain free access to his estate if we wanted to solve the death of Chelion. We had to talk to the servants, establish alibis for the time of his death, investigate motives, find out who might have held a grudge against the scribe, and so on.

And in the end we would probably face our most difficult task, namely to try to convince Dexippa that her son had died a natural death—as unthinkable as that might seem to her.

Layla had perhaps been a bit too determined, too brisk in her dealings with Latobios. So for the time being, I took a different approach and changed the subject, even if it might be quite conspicuous. Back to neutral ground, so to speak.

"I am led to you by a special request, honored Latobios," I began, "apart from the fact that we would like to hear your opinion about the witch Luscinia, as Layla has already indicated. It's regarding your expertise when it comes to horses."

"Oh yeah?" At the mention of the word *horses,* the man's jaw muscles immediately relaxed. From one moment to the next, he already looked a lot friendlier.

So I had judged him correctly.

"Yes," I affirmed. "It's because my best riding horse is getting a bit long in the tooth. A breeding of my brother—of whom you may have heard, because he is a horse connoisseur of the first rank, just like yourself. I am attached to my steed, as it has always served me most faithfully, but unfortunately I will soon have to look for a new one I'm afraid."

I told him my brother's name—without mentioning that Morcan and I had not exchanged a word for years. My brother's horse breeding was prestigious, and his steeds were even in great demand by the Roman legions.

"Morcan is your *brother*?" asked Latobios incredulously. Now even a small smile showed momentarily on his face, and he seemed to notice me properly for the first time. "Why didn't you say so in the first place? Morcan—he's a tribal lord in the north, isn't he? Not far from Vindobona. Of course I know his name. He must be a remarkable man, even though I have not yet met him in person. Quite outstanding! His breedings speak for themselves, even if he puts emphasis on strength and endurance in his animals. Whereas with my horses, naturally, I have always been concerned with light-footedness and maximum speed. I would be delighted if you could introduce me to Morcan, when the opportunity arises."

"I'm sure you will, and I'll be happy to," I lied.

"Now of course I've spoken to him about my new mount," I continued—which was also a fictitious claim. Yes, I didn't even have a need for a new steed, because my best stallion was barely eight years old. But the favor of Latobios could only be won by this subterfuge.

"But I've heard that you are even more of an expert on horses than Morcan," I continued hypocritically, "and that your animals are especially famous for their speed. And that is what matters to me, do you understand? I want to ride a fiery stallion that can leave all the others behind. Perhaps you could sell me a suitable animal?"

"I don't trade my horses," Latobios said. "I breed only for my own pleasure. After all, I'm retired, and don't need any more income."

There it was again, an indication of just how wealthy Latobios was. The typical behavior of a nouveau riche.

I did not know this man's parents' occupations, but they had not belonged to Vindobona's elite, and had certainly not been millionaires. Real members of the moneyed aristocracy, such as my friend Marcellus—who had been born with a silver spoon in his mouth—never spoke about their wealth. For them, it went without saying that they could buy anything their hearts desired, and they would never have boasted of their wealth to their friends or even to strangers. It was all a given.

"Certainly. I understand," I said quickly. "Well, then maybe you can at least give me some good advice. What should I look for when buying my new mount?"

Latobios hesitated for a moment. Then he said, "Yes, fine. Why not?"

I guess I had to add a little more to truly find favor with him.

"I have also heard that you are a great connoisseur and lover of the finest silverware," I added. In this case, it was to my advantage that the man was one of Vindobona's more famous sons. As I've said, people loved to talk about him, and I knew a lot about his preferences, even though I hadn't set foot in his villa until today.

"That's true," he said with eyebrows raised curiously. "But what makes you think of that now?"

I had him on the hook.

"I'm a trader," I said without mincing my words. "In luxury goods. I can get you some particularly choice pieces, if you're interested."

I mentioned the names of several silversmiths whose works were in great demand in Rome, and raved at length to the charioteer about food bowls and drinking cups that came from the manufactories of these artists.

It would not be easy to actually procure such precious items, no matter what price I named for them, but I could play for time. After all, Vindobona was not exactly a suburb of the mighty Rome. Transport to our province took half an eternity—and besides that, precious cargo of all kinds could fall victim to a band of robbers, and never reach its destination. So I already had a suitable excuse for the ultimate failure of a business transaction between the retired chariot racer and myself, no matter what treasures I might hold out to him in order to win his sympathy.

My words did not miss their mark. Now, finally, Latobios smiled. He looked only at me, ignoring Layla completely, but in the next breath he invited us both to dinner. Apparently he did have some basic manners, when he was interested in showing his good side. And a self-respecting gentleman could not simply invite a visitor to stay and at the same time put his companion out on the street.

"Stay and be my guests tonight," he said in a suddenly unctuous tone. "I have had a sumptuous meal prepared, for I am expecting another visitor, an old friend who is dear to me. It would please me if you would join us. We could take this opportunity to talk about your new horse, Thanar—and about my silver tableware. It is true that I am a passionate collector. And no price is too high for an exceptional piece."

Layla and I were only too happy to accept his invitation, even though we could not move freely around the house in the hours leading up to the evening meal as we had hoped.

Latobios led us to one of his gardens, where a servant served us sweet treats and chilled honey wine. Layla and I had no choice but to let ourselves be pampered, and wait for the promised evening meal.

I asked one of the house slaves to bring word to Telephus and our coachman that we would not be starting our journey home until later that evening.

At first we did not gain access to Hersilia, the wife of the racing driver, and we did not succeed in making inquiries among the servants who tended to our needs.

Instead, Latobios sent us his son, a rather slight youth named Smertius, who was perhaps eighteen years old, to regale us with erudite conversation. He had a tangled mop of dark hair, large green eyes, and a sparse, rather unkempt-looking growth of beard. He was worlds apart from his father's athletic physique and successful appearance.

Smertius was a studious young man, which he emphasized as often as his father spoke about his fortune, and he had apparently devoted himself to philosophy with the same passion as Latobios to his steeds. He enjoyed all too much, for my taste, to hear himself talk.

The young man was indeed educated, you had to give him that, but he was not an entertaining narrator or even a great rhetorician.

I had to stifle a yawn several times while listening to what he had to say, and poor Layla, while being amiable as always and nodding smilingly at the appropriate parts of Smertius's monologue, also looked like she was going to die of boredom at any moment.

Smertius seemed to admire his father very much, because apart from the philosophical wisdom with which he was trying to regale us, he spoke several times about Latobios's brilliant achievements at the Circus Maximus and at other famous racetracks, and what a brave and outstanding man his father was.

Very well, Layla and I practiced patience. At dinner, I would talk to Latobios about his experience with Luscinia, the witch who had supposedly healed one of his steeds—I made a point of doing that. I had to make sure that Alma would not be in any danger if we actually did lead her to this magician. And after that, hopefully, the opportunity would arise to pursue our work as Detectores, as far as the death of the slave Chelion was concerned.

That was our plan, at least.

VII

The other guest who had been invited to dinner at Latobios's *domus* turned out to be a medicus named Lucius Avernus. He was a tall, handsome man who dressed himself in the manner of the Celts, and wore a patterned shirt and tight-fitting trousers. His hair was midnight black, his skin a warm shade of brown, though not as dark as Layla's.

I suspected that, despite the Latin name and Celtic dress, he came from Greece, as was often the case with doctors. Or perhaps he was from Asia Minor. The Imperium Romanum is a melting pot of the most diverse cultures, and every free man—or freedman—can pick out the elements from this mixture that suit him best. I myself am a good example of this. A Romanized barbarian, so to speak....

But back to Avernus. He was a middle-aged man, as they say, so he was about the same age as Latobios or me. The most striking thing about him was his set of teeth: his jaw was so powerful that it made me think of one of Latobios's proud stallions.

In a fit of silliness, the following crossed my mind: *is Latobios perhaps such close friends with this Avernus because he reminds him of his beloved four-legged friends?* I really was in a strange mood lately: tense and almost desperate because of Alma on the one hand, but as obviously childish and silly as ever on the other. Well, perhaps the latter was my way of somehow coping with the former.

Besides the doctor, Smertius also attended the meal with us, along with Hersilia, his mother, who had dressed up so elaborately that her beauty almost dazzled me.

Latobios drew our attention to her lovely appearance—not that that was necessary. One would have had to be blind to overlook Hersilia.

"Is my beloved wife not the most beautiful woman in all of Vindobona?" the charioteer said, as soon as we had settled down on the dining couches.

Hersilia gracefully bowed her head in thanks for this compliment, only to fall completely silent and sink into a depressed haze as dinner progressed.

It turned out that Latobios's friend, Avernus, served as a doctor in the camp hospital at Vindobona, and Layla knew the man by sight. From the way he kept looking at her in wonder during dinner, she was also known to him, and he was no doubt well aware that she was the camp commander's mistress. Certainly he was wondering what she was doing in the company of a barbarian merchant in the house of Latobios. But he was too polite to put his curiosity into words.

Avernus seemed to really be a close friend of our host's. The retired charioteer probably knew him so well that he soon noticed his apparently uncharacteristic behavior this evening.

"Something is wrong with you, my dear Avernus," he said suddenly. "Is it not so?"

I had not noticed anything unusual. In my eyes, the doctor behaved exactly as one might expect from a guest with perfect manners. But I was not as familiar with the man as Latobios clearly was.

"What troubles you, my friend?" he continued to probe, while some of his slaves laid out a sumptuous selection of dishes—all on magnificent silver plate, of course.

One might have thought that three more guests were expected for dinner, judging from the sheer amount of food on the tables. There was pheasant, liver and black pudding, a fish with snow-white meat, roasted thrushes, baked snails, pork ragout and wine rolls—I must confess that my mouth was watering just looking at it all.

Avernus, on the other hand, made a frustrated hand gesture. His friend had apparently hit the mark as far as his conflicted mood was concerned. And he seemingly wanted to get the grief off his chest, too.

He opened his lips, murmured something that sounded like, "You're right, my friend," but then broke off and squinted over at Layla. He was probably considering how freely he might be able to speak in front of the legate's companion.

After a moment's reflection, he came to the conclusion that he had nothing to hide, and the next moment he was already starting to report: "Ah—a patient of mine in the legionary camp is worrying me," he complained, his face distorted with sorrow. "Sergius Martianus is a deserving centurion and quite a splendid fellow—but as of late, he is afflicted with a kind of madness against which I am powerless. I have tried just about everything, and yet...." He shrugged his shoulders, and pressed his lips together.

Latobios pushed a silver wine cup that one of the slaves had just poured over to him. On the side of the vessel, facing toward me, was a centaur with a huge drinking horn.

"Here. Strengthen yourself, my friend," said the charioteer. "A noble Falernian that will warm your soul. What has happened to the man, then? To this Martianus?" he added. "Had he experienced terrible things in the face of the enemy? Surely your legion has not fought in a battle for years, or am I mistaken?"

"No, you are quite right," said Avernus. "Fortunately we live in a time of peace, and no enemy dares try to cross the Limes. And even if they did—the most fearsome foe probably couldn't harm Martianus. He is one of the bravest men I know."

"What is it, then, that has brought him to his knees?" asked Latobios with undisguised curiosity. "And how does this madness of which you speak manifest itself?"

Avernus hesitated for a long moment. Then he said, "It was the death of his only son that threw him so badly off course. When he lost the boy, he fell into a deep melancholy ... and that was only the beginning."

"Is melancholy not due to an excess of black bile?" interposed Latobios's son Smertius. "And can it not be at least alleviated, if not entirely dispelled, by cupping, by tried and true herbal remedies, and foods?"

Until now Smertius had not spoken a word, but he had followed the conversation of the two older men with obvious attention. Now he seemed to want to shine with his great erudition before his father's guests.

Avernus nodded. "Quite so, Smertius," he said, praising the young man, "and of course those were my first actions. Unlike some of my esteemed colleagues, I do not consider melancholy a punishment of the gods. Martianus, at any rate, is certainly not guilty of anything that would have incurred the wrath of the immortals."

"Certainly not," I said quickly. I didn't know the said Martianus, but he sounded like a man who had his heart in the right place. And surely there was nothing wrong in mourning a lost son. I knew only too well how much the death of a loved one could throw one off course.

VIII

"It got worse after that," Avernus continued with his report. "Martianus's condition deteriorated with each passing day, no matter how hard I tried to care for him. He began to neglect his duties, and to treat his subordinates unfairly ... downright bullying them, if I'm honest. His character changed, and not for the better. He became withdrawn, moody, and belligerent towards the most harmless fellows, and in time unequivocally paranoid. He became more and more convinced that Marcus, his beloved little son, had been murdered, and that it was his duty as a father to bring the murderer to the cross. By now he is completely beside himself—and only yesterday I had to doctor him because he had made cuts on his arms with his own knife. Afterwards he couldn't even remember having done it, and didn't have the slightest idea what had driven him to it."

"That sounds terrible," Layla said sympathetically. "The poor man."

Avernus nodded, then finally reached for the wine cup that Latobios had offered him. He took a hearty sip and closed his eyes for a brief moment, enjoying the effects.

"Well, thank you for hearing me out," he said with a faint nod of his head. "It feels good to be able to tell nice people my woes. But I don't want to spoil your evening, so let's—"

Latobios raised his hands defensively and interrupted his friend. "Not at all, my dear. A sorrow shared is a sorrow halved; you will always find an open ear with me. And besides, I may know a remedy for your problem."

Avernus uttered a sound of astonishment, which Latobios acknowledged with a satisfied smile. Then the former charioteer pointed at me with his hand.

"Thanar is my guest tonight for the same reason," he explained to the medicus. "He, too, faces an insoluble medical problem—concerning his beloved, is that not so?" he prompted me.

I nodded in agreement. I wanted to tell the medic about the witch Luscinia, in whom I placed my last hope regarding Alma's healing. But that was not necessary, because Latobios immediately started on that himself. He began to tell his friend about his sick horse, which had been cured so spectacularly by Luscinia.

"Fulgur is the best steed I have left from my active time in the circus. A horse the likes of which you only find once in a decade. He always ran on the outside right of the team, so he had to be the fastest in the curves," he added, addressing me. Apparently he assumed that, as a provincial, I had little familiarity with chariot racing. Vindobona did not have a circus to call its own.

Turning to Avernus, Latobios added, "Fulgur is only eight years old, but he has already suffered some injuries and has worked very hard for me. Then, a few weeks ago, he suddenly didn't want to eat from one day to the next. He lay down more and more often, and in the end he wouldn't get up at all. And he seemed to be in terrible pain—"

He shook his head as though he could drive away the awful memory with it. "Well, to cut a long story short, I left no stone unturned to find a cure for Fulgur. I spent vast sums on every sort of expert, but none of them knew anything useful in the end. The horse seemed to be getting closer and closer to death. The slave in charge of my stables finally recommended a witch, Luscinia. He had heard of her deeds, described her to me as a miracle worker ... and by then I was truly desperate. I would have literally done anything."

"A witch, you say?" Avernus literally spat out the words. "You can't be serious, old friend!"

Latobios grinned condescendingly. "I understand you only too well, because at first I thought exactly the same way. But as I said, I didn't know what else to do—I would have tried anything. I would have descended into the Underworld myself to save my faithful Fulgur from death."

"How exactly did Luscinia manage to help your horse?" Layla interposed. Now we were on exactly the subject that interested us so much. The all-important question: *do we really dare to take Alma to this miracle healer?*

"What she did exactly, I cannot say," Latobios replied. "She cast some sort of spell, poured a potion for Fulgur ... and finally told me that an ill-wishing spell, designed to harm, had been cast on the poor animal. It was a curse that was probably still upon him from our days together on the racetrack. One of my competitors had probably wanted to defeat me in this way. I don't have to tell you how frequently even the biggest circus celebrities like to use damaging magic. They curse their opponents and their horses, wish them pain and wounds and call the greatest of mental torment down on their necks. They do not even shy away from summoning demons and the dark gods to harm their competitors, so that they may take the prize money and gain fame for themselves. I myself never did such things, of course!" he quickly added. "I really didn't need to."

I didn't believe a word he said. Latobios was certainly not squeamish when it came to winning a competition. He was an ambitious and a very proud man.

"Luscinia was finally able to banish the curse that was upon Fulgur," he continued, "and took a pretty sesterce from me to do it. Not that I care; just one day later, my stallion was back to his old self. And that's the only thing that counts for me, so I can recommend this Luscinia without reservation. To you, Thanar, and also to you, my dear Avernus."

He turned to his friend with a serious look. "You also have nothing to lose, it seems to me, just as was the case with my horse. If you want to save your patient, this Martianus, from complete insanity, I think you have no choice but to engage Luscinia's services. Isn't that so? And what could possibly go wrong? You're not risking anything, and he'll only get worse, regardless."

You're not risking anything? As far as that was concerned, I strongly disagreed, but kept the thought to myself. If you confide in a witch, you risk incurring the wrath of the gods. And the worldly punishments we might face were also a very real threat.

To prove that a witch used only healing magic was almost impossible. Besides, the talk regarding Luscinia was anything but positive. If you were denounced for having hired a dark sorceress, you could lose your head in the worst case—and not only in the symbolic sense! Whoever might even be suspected of working or commissioning damaging magic could quickly find himself on a cross or stake at the next fork in the road, or with his neck beneath the executioner's sword.

Avernus lapsed into a brooding silence. He ate a piece of fish, then a large portion of the pork ragout, and seemed to ponder dully to himself.

Finally he reached for his napkin, cleaned his lips and said, "You're right, Latobios. I do indeed have nothing to lose—or rather, Martianus doesn't. I see no other way out for him, so I will suggest he seeks out this Luscinia. Let's see what he thinks of it."

As dinner was drawing to a close, and I had perhaps already indulged a little too heavily in the wine, Smertius suddenly took the floor. Eager as a favorite slave, he offered to show me Fulgur, his father's magnificent horse, which had been so miraculously cured by the witch.

"Father is truly not only the greatest of charioteers, but also the best horse breeder far and wide," he exclaimed with fervor.

Smertius might already be an adult, but at that moment he seemed to me like a little child, vying for his father's attention—and even his love—with his passionate admiration.

Before I could accept Smertius's offer, Latobios intervened.

"I will give you a tour of my stables myself, and introduce you to Fulgur, Thanar," he announced. "And I will also show you some of my other steeds on this occasion. Afterwards, you'll be in the know regarding what to look for when buying your new riding horse. And then we'll have a few cups together, won't we, Avernus?" He turned back to the medicus. "Will you accompany us to the stables?"

The doctor readily agreed.

The master of the house seemed to have forgotten my offer concerning the silverware, but that was just fine by me. After all, I had not come to his villa to do business.

Smertius seemed disappointed that he had been passed over, but did not contradict his father. He left the room without a word as Latobios rose and we followed him toward the stables.

Layla stayed behind at Hersilia's side—which was excellent. While we men devoted ourselves to the horses, she would have free rein to investigate the house—and the death of Chelion.

IX

If I hadn't feigned leaden fatigue at some point, Latobios's stable tour would probably have taken up the entire night.

He never stopped talking, showing me every single mare, stallion and gelding—and he really did have an enormous number of them.

Finally I succeeded in pleading weariness, and Latobios returned to the house with Avernus to pay homage to the pleasures of Bacchus for a while.

We met Smertius as soon as we'd left the stable building. It seemed to me that Latobios's son had been waiting around just to join us again. His father—absorbed in conversation with Avernus—paid him no attention at all. The two men walked past without even looking at him.

So without further ado, he walked up to me, put on a smile, and asked how I liked his father's steeds. "Aren't they magnificent animals?" he said eagerly.

I confirmed this. Actually, I was quite tired and wanted to return home as soon as possible, but it seemed to me a good opportunity to hear Smertius's views on the magical healing that Luscinia had performed on Latobios's favorite horse.

If it were possible I would have gotten confirmation from a thousand people that Luscinia was indeed only a healer, and a very good one at that—not a dark magician who damned her clients forever in the eyes of the gods because she used forbidden powers. I was still struggling with myself as to whether I should really bring Alma to this woman. Were we truly so desperate?

So I asked Smertius the question that so tormented me, but learned nothing that Latobios had not already recounted.

Smertius emphasized that Luscinia had acted quickly and confidently, and that Fulgur the racehorse had been back on his feet in no time. He also assured me that Luscinia's assistant, Sagana, was also a great sorceress, and was unjustly overshadowed by her mistress. Apparently the two women had come to the house together to treat Fulgur.

"If I may ask, Thanar," he added, "why are you so interested in witchcraft? Are you like me? Do you find it fascinating?"

"Yes, I do," I affirmed. Then I made a flimsy excuse and finally took my leave.

Smertius disappeared in the direction of the house—presumably in the hope of joining the two older men and scoring points with his erudition in their male conversation.

Relationships between fathers and sons are sometimes complicated, but it also seemed to me that Latobios did not exactly shine in the role of being a father. If I had a son, I told myself, I would treat him with the utmost attention and esteem, and I would certainly not prefer any horse to him, no matter how remarkable it might be. Could I still hope at some point to begin a family of my own?

I found Layla in the front yard of the estate, where she had joined Telephus and our coachman.

The two men were in the company of one of Latobios's older grooms, and as I joined them, I just caught Layla unobtrusively yet pointedly asking the man about Chelion's death.

However, he did not want to say more than that the unfortunate scribe must surely have had an enemy who—with the help of black magic—had brought him to his sudden death. He even repeated just how healthy Chelion had appeared prior to his demise.

"Our master should not have brought that witch into the house!" the man shouted, his impetuous gestures giving emphasis to his words. However, when he caught sight of me, he fell silent and scurried off.

"Now you've scared him away," Layla welcomed me with mock reproach in her voice.

"Sorry," I muttered, "but he didn't seem to have any really useful information in any case."

"You're right about that. I've been hearing similar things from almost all the residents of the house and the servants as well."

"You questioned them all?" I asked incredulously. All of the *familia*—the slaves, servants, and farmhands—in the house of Latobios certainly amounted to a small army.

"Not all of them," Layla said. "Many moved out of my way, some I didn't even meet because they were going about their business in other parts of the house...."

She fell silent and seemed to be brooding darkly. Apparently she had discovered something that was worth thinking about.

"Let's go home," I suggested, helping Layla climb into the carriage. I would find out what was going through her mind on the way.

Telephus took a seat on the front bench next to the

coachman, probably in an effort to give us some privacy—but that was not necessary. Our conversation on the ride home was not romantic, not even friendly, but revolved exclusively around the death of the slave Chelion and what she had learned.

"I first escorted Hersilia to her chambers," Layla began her account of her after-dinner activities. "I gave her one of my herbal mixtures to lift her from her dull mood, but without any real success, I'm afraid."

Layla had already set out her own garden on my land some time ago, where she'd planted medicinal herbs—but also some of the most diverse poisonous plants available, which she wanted to study closely. Therefore the garden was located near my house, not near the Legate Palace of Marcellus. A poison garden in the middle of the legion camp would not have gone down well at all, as one can easily imagine. Cultivating deadly plants was as much a capital offense in the Roman Empire as practicing black magic, because of how one could use them.

"Have you been able to find out what is troubling Hersilia? Or is she by nature such a quiet and melancholy character?" I could hardly imagine that of such a beautiful woman. On the other hand, a person didn't have to be happy just because the gods had gifted him or her with good looks.

Layla shrugged. "She didn't really open up to me, I'm afraid. She stressed several times that everything was alright, that she was fine. She was 'just a little tired,' she assured me. But when I brought up Luscinia and her magical powers, the subject seemed to instill great fear in her."

"But Luscinia only cured Latobios's horse, didn't she?" I

said. "She only brought about good things in this house. So why do they fear her so much?"

"Well, that's probably due to Chelion's death," Layla said. "I think they put it down to a spell or curse. I met a house slave, a Gaul named Olivia, who declared that he had been struck down by dark magic. It was she who found his body, in a corridor near the kitchen. And she swears with all her heart that she had passed by there only a short time before, and that there was definitely no dead body on the floor at that time, least of all of Chelion."

"And what's so surprising about that to them? Surely Chelion must have died in the intervening time?"

"Well, she claims his body was already ice cold when she found it—which is exactly why she believes he was killed by a spell. If he had died of natural causes, he should still have been warm when she passed the corridor for the second time."

"Hmm. That is indeed strange," I said, relenting.

But then I had an idea. "He may have been dead for some time when this Olivia person found him," I speculated. "He may have died in another place, after all. In another part of the house? Someone could have dumped his body in that hallway, though I can't think of a reason why."

"That someone would have to be Chelion's killer then, wouldn't they?" said Layla. "Who else would have a motive to take his body away, and dump it somewhere else?"

"Which would mean that Chelion actually was killed," I muttered to myself. I had not seriously believed that until now.

"Maybe Chelion died in the killer's room, or at least near to it," Layla said, "and that's why the killer had to move his body somewhere else, to avoid suspicion. Or maybe he wanted to disguise the time of his victim's death."

"To have an alibi for the time of the crime?" I asked.

Layla nodded. "Quite possibly."

She looked over to the houses of the civilian part of the city, which were just passing us on the right. Then, however, she turned back to me.

"It seemed to me that this Olivia was particularly devoted to Chelion. She was fighting back tears when I approached her regarding the dead man—and her eyes had looked reddened to me before."

"Was there anything she could tell you about him that might indicate a motive for murder? Or even a perpetrator?"

"Hmm, she wasn't accusing anyone in particular, if that's what you mean. Even though there would have to have been a client behind the witchcraft spell she spoke of."

"So in her opinion, Chelion had no enemies in the house? Or in the city?"

"On the contrary; from what Olivia and the rest of Latobios's servants told me about him, he was a very well-respected man. Handsome, educated, always friendly, even to the lower-ranking slaves in the house. And he also seemed to be popular with the masters. Olivia thought he always had enough money to afford small pleasures in the city. A hot sausage, a mug of beer—and he was probably generous to others in the process."

"Then Latobios, his wife, and his son must be spendthrifts as far as allowances to their servants are concerned," I said. "For how else would a slave like Chelion come to have such a full purse?"

"He could have been pursuing some secret business," Layla suggested, "that ended up being his undoing?"

However, it seemed to me that she put forward this theory without any real conviction.

"As for the money, I guess we'll have to go back to the question of why he couldn't buy his freedom. Or if he wasn't allowed to," I said. "Do you think Latobios was telling us the truth? That he wouldn't have minded releasing Chelion for the right amount? Or was he lying to us?"

"It seemed to me he was honest with us. Why should he have tried to fool us?" said Layla.

"Hmm, well. What if Chelion knew something about Latobios, for example? After all, he served him for a very long time, didn't he? And these charioteers are not squeamish fellows in general, and neither is Latobios in particular, it seems to me. Perhaps he was guilty of something in his younger days that could cause him serious trouble now if it came to light? Maybe that's why he wanted Chelion in his house forever, where he had him under his control? Therefore he didn't release him, but treated him well even so. Gave him regular lavish tips."

The theory didn't sound bad at all, I thought. But Layla didn't seem very convinced.

I added one more: "What if things somehow got out of hand in the end?" I suggested. "Maybe Chelion was demanding more and more money for his silence as time went on ... and Latobios, therefore, decided to get rid of him forever. He could have hired the witch to kill Chelion—"

Layla frowned. "It can't be ruled out," she muttered, "but it would be a completely unnecessary effort if you're only going to kill one of your own slaves."

Then she looked out into the night again. On the right hand side, a rather poor row of houses was stretching along, completely in the dark. There was no money for lamp oil left in these dwellings.

Layla brooded silently for a while. Only when we rumbled through a pothole did it seem to rouse her again. She looked at me.

"Olivia said something else that might be significant," she explained. "Chelion was said to be particularly fond of a youngster in the house, a slave named Timor who worked as an errand boy. She didn't say it directly, but it seemed to me she was implying that the two were connected by more than mere friendship."

I shrugged my shoulders. That the members of a large slave *familia* indulged in certain love affairs or even more serious relationships among themselves was nothing unusual. And many a man preferred the strong arms of an attractive younger male to those of a girl.

I dropped Layla off at the legionary camp, and Telephus accompanied her through the gate as a matter of course. He would spend the night in the legate's palace, as he had been often doing lately, as if Layla really needed a personal bodyguard here, in this most secure of places. It seemed to me that the former gladiator had really taken a fancy to my beautiful Nubian. Or rather, to Marcellus's beautiful Nubian.

I left Layla behind, in body as well as in my mind, crossed

the Danubius River as fast as my horses would run, and returned to the woman who was now mine—if I did not soon lose her forever to the darkness, at least....

Nemesis the gladiatrix welcomed me in the atrium.

"How is Alma?" I asked as soon as I had greeted her.

A small smile flashed across the arena fighter's face. "She was able to sleep a little in the afternoon," she said, "and now she is in the library. We just had a new work by a young poet read to us. His name has slipped my mind—"

I knew that Nemesis was not a bookworm like Alma or Layla were. But she was a loyal friend and stood by Alma, no matter if she had to listen to some poetry she was only slightly interested in.

I followed the gladiatrix into the library to embrace my beloved.

X

The following afternoon we met the witch, Luscinia. As agreed, we once again visited Sagana, the assistant of the great master, in Rufius's rest house. We paid the agreed sum and were then accompanied by her to a wooded area south of the civilian part of the city, where Luscinia had set up her secret camp.

The witch had a surprisingly imposing appearance. She was not the sort of woman one might have called beautiful, but her aspect, her movements and the sparkle in her gray-blue eyes spoke of power. Of power—and the self-confidence that came with it.

She had long blonde hair and a voluptuous body that paid testament to plentiful meals and a soft bed for the night. Even though she might have already passed forty she looked like a much younger woman, bursting with vitality. It seemed to me that her roots lay somewhere in the far north as did those of Alma, but she spoke the same cultured Latin that any fine Roman lady might have.

She had us sit down in a place covered with blankets and pillows in the shade of a huge oak tree, where she took to silently eyeing Layla, Telephus, and me.

Sagana, her assistant, stayed in the background, and an older man who was one of the witch's servants took over watering our horses, and then joined our coachman for a chat.

A short distance away from the large oak, several tents had been set up in the shade of some other trees—the dwelling of the witch, I suspected. Even further away were two carriages, and several well-fed horses were grazing in a small clearing. Everything seemed ... how shall I say it? Idyllic? Nothing dark clung to this place, at least, nothing that I could have perceived after hearing the tales of the dread cloud over Latobios's estate. I was filled with relief.

When Luscinia finally seemed ready to begin the session, she first asked our desire—even though Sagana had surely described to her what brought us here in advance.

Telephus took the floor. He pointed to his eyes with his fingertips, and spoke of his failing eyesight. "Would the wise Luscinia perhaps know a means to improve my eyesight again? Or at least to stop the deterioration?" Telephus spoke softly, in a tone of voice I had never heard the former gladiator use. Luscinia seemed to inspire great awe in him.

She listened to him in silence, not taking her eyes off him, and when she finally spoke up, she said something unexpected: "It seems to me you're not the only one here seeking my help."

Telephus opened his mouth, but not a word passed his lips. I was equally astonished. Was this a sample of Luscinia's clairvoyant powers?

She laughed suddenly, as unaffected and as lively as a young girl. "You don't have to possess second sight for that bit of intuition, my esteemed guests," she cried. "Two rich people, finely dressed, and traveling in an expensive coach, accompanying a simple guard to see me? You may be friends with your dear Telephus, and very concerned about his eyesight ... but such an escort seems a bit excessive even so. So tell me, what is it that brings you to me in truth? What is your desire?"

"Telephus's eyesight really is—"

That was as far as I got. Luscinia silenced me with a commanding wave of her hand.

"His eyesight is something I'm going to get right onto, so you can consider it done."

She beckoned Sagana over, and the assistant bent over her in such a way that her long dark hair fell like a curtain between us and the witch. The two women whispered briefly to each other, of which I could just barely understand a few words. It seemed that Luscinia was giving her assistant instructions for a recipe that she was to carry out.

Finally, Sagana hurried away at a run, heading for one of the tents, and disappeared inside.

"Sagana will mix an elixir for you," Luscinia told Telephus. "You will use it twice a day, at sunrise and sunset. It will stop the fading of your eyesight, or even improve your sight—if the gods are kind to you."

Telephus bowed sitting down, as deeply and reverently as if he were facing the emperor himself. "I thank you, master! What do I owe you for the medicine?"

I braced myself to hear a sum over a hundred sesterces—in view of what we had already paid in advance for Luscinia to receive us at all. But to my astonishment, she only mentioned a price of twenty sesterces—and added that the elixir would last for several months.

Telephus beamed with joy and uttered a torrent of thanks.

Luscinia nodded at him, once again sympathetically, then

fixed her gaze on me. However, she finally directed her words at Layla, whom she had been insistently eyeing the whole time. Layla's night-black skin and her equally dark hair, which she wore pinned up in a complicated style in the manner of the Roman matrons, seemed to fascinate Luscinia. And she'd probably picked up on the attentive look with which Layla followed her every move, and her every utterance.

"Now, will you tell me what brings you both to me?" she asked. "The healing of your friend will take several weeks. My elixir is strong, but it is not brewed by the hands of the gods. Do you really want to wait that long to introduce me to the other person who is seeking help? The one who is even more dear to both of you than your friend here? It seems to me that this person is in great pain. I can read the despair and worry in your faces."

Even though she directed her words to Layla, it was I myself who spontaneously spoke up.

"It is my beloved who is in terrible straits," I said. "But I don't want to put her in danger—"

I hesitated; far be it from me to offend Luscinia, but I could not silence the concerns that were gnawing at me incessantly.

"*Danger*?" repeated Luscinia in surprise. "From me?"

I nodded, a little embarrassed.

Then I took heart and said straightforwardly, "You may not have been in Vindobona for very long, but your reputation already precedes you. Your healing spells are said to be of great efficacy."

"But...?" Luscinia frowned.

"Well, you're also said to do—well, darker things. Spells that aren't for healing. Deeds for which some seek to place the blame on you."

If I had snubbed Luscinia with my words, she did not let on. She merely lapsed into a dull, brooding attitude, until she finally raised her head and affirmed to me with what seemed to be sincere fervor that everything dark was far from her.

"I never do any harm; I only work for the good of the people," she announced in a strong voice. "But I know that some often talk badly about me. I am blamed for things I truly have had no involvement in. This is not the first time I have experienced this."

She shook her head in frustration. "But enough about me, let's talk about the woman who needs my help. Won't you describe her torment to me in more detail?"

What could I say? I intuitively trusted the witch and her words. Thus I began to describe Alma's suffering to her, without holding anything back.

"She can't sleep anymore," I began. "She hasn't been able to for weeks. As soon as she lies down and closes her eyes, she's haunted by the most horrific dream creatures. That may not sound particularly extraordinary; after all, most of us probably go through a nightmare now and then. But in Alma's case, these night terrors seem to be chasing after her very life, trying to drive her out of her mind—or worse. In the dream, there are images that haunt her. She sees herself dying, in a hundred different ways: at the stake, on the cross, in the arena, in a conflagration, in the floods of the Danubius. Or rather, she *experiences* her death, and with every one of her senses—over and over again."

I shook my head, trying to swallow the cold lump that had

formed in my throat. "The dreams really are putting her through the wringer, like she's in the hands of the worst torturer. And every night, without ceasing. She has hardly any strength left; indeed, she no longer even dares to close her eyes."

"And this sleep deprivation is debilitating to her, isn't it?" said Luscinia. "On and on until she will be at death's very door." She sounded most understanding.

"That's right," I confirmed. "Alma is only a shadow of her former self. She is brave, fighting the dreams, but to no avail."

I described to the witch all the efforts we had already made to free Alma from her awful night terrors. I spoke of healers, doctors, priests, astrologers and oracles—but none of them had been able to help us.

Finally I took a break, and began talking about what might be the cause of Alma's hideous dreams.

"The torment began a few days after a nasty incident," I said. "Alma was kidnapped by a gang of robbers, because of me."

"Because of me too," Layla interjected. "We ... had been on the trail of a murderer, and his henchmen kidnapped Alma."

I added: "We finally succeeded in saving her through a ruse, and the fiends received their just punishment. At first, Alma seemed able to put it all behind her, the martyrdom she had suffered. I had the impression that she had taken no harm ... but then these nightmares assailed her like an evil spell."

Luscinia furrowed her brow.

Layla mentioned some herbs from which she had already brewed potions and elixirs for Alma. These had also had no real effect.

Luscinia nodded sympathetically at Layla. "Not a bad

approach—you have acted wisely. But something stronger is probably needed." The next moment, the witch jumped to her feet.

"Wait a moment," she said, then hurried toward the tent wherein Sagana had disappeared earlier.

It was a long time before she returned. She handed me a small silver pendant, an amulet on a ribbon that could be tied around the neck.

It was in the shape of a phallus—which wasn't surprising to me. The male member is a symbol of good health, of strength, and of flourishing life. It is known that it can ward off evil. Nevertheless, such an amulet seemed to me too simple, too weak to be able to save Alma.

Luscinia probably saw my disappointment.

"I have imbued this amulet with my strongest spells," she assured me, "and I will also send you a special fur blanket that will protect from fears and dangers. Wrap your beloved in it at night, or whenever she tries to find sleep. I hope to finish the blanket by tomorrow or the day after, and I will have it brought to you then."

She had me describe where my house was located.

I thanked the witch, but without any real enthusiasm.

I didn't know what I'd expected, either. She charged me sixty sesterces for the amulet and the blanket she was still making for me, and I paid without protest.

"If these two spells do not help," Luscinia told me in parting, "you will have to bring your Alma to me. She is still able to travel, isn't she?"

"She will come," I said. "My carriage is comfortable and fast, and the road here is not unbearably long."

It was clear to me that I could not demand a house call from Luscinia, which was in all our interests. To reach my house on the north bank of the Danubius, she would at least have had to cross the camp suburb, and would probably have come closer to the legionary camp—and thus to Roman law—than was good for her.

Latobios's house was a bit out of the way, not even within the walls of the civilian city, and there had been no choice but a home visit for his terminally ill horse. Fulgur had no longer been fit for transport.

But I had been able to see for myself what a terrible impression Luscinia's visit to the charioteer's villa had left. And who was really able to say what connection the death of the slave Chelion might have with her appearance in the end. She seemed all too well aware of the stories people told about her.

I could not risk anything similar within my own four walls. Such an atmosphere of fear and mistrust as I had felt in the racing driver's house would be fatal for Alma, of that I was sure.

Telephus received a small glass vial with the elixir for his eyes. I safely stowed the phallic amulet in the pouch I was carrying, then we took our leave of the witch.

"I really had imagined worse of her," I said to Layla as soon as we were back in our car. "She does seem pretty harmless, don't you think?"

"Oh no. She's definitely not harmless," Layla contradicted me. "She's a very powerful woman, I'm sure of it."

"Good, agreed. Powerful. But not evil. Honorable, it seems to me. Considerate, even."

Thereupon I once again reaped one of Layla's famous sphinx's looks.

I asked her if she wanted to spend the evening at my house, since Marcellus was away, but she declined. "I want to go back to the villa of Latobios," she said, "and talk there with this boy Timor, whom Olivia had described to me."

"The slave boy who is said to have been Chelion's lover?"

"That's the one. Maybe he knows something about the death of the scribe, or about his life before he died. Whether Chelion kept dark secrets, or made any enemies—"

XI

The witch's silver phallic amulet—as precious as it might look—proved useless to Alma, at least on that first night.

At first I was hopeful, because right after dinner—and after she had put on the amulet—she was overcome by tiredness. I carried her in my arms to her bedchamber, laid her gently on the bed, and then watched by her side for quite a while. She slept quietly and peacefully, and I dared to hope....

But then the worst nightmares came over her again. She screamed, grabbed her throat as if she were suffocating, and retched pitifully.

I didn't ask, but I suspected that they had hanged her in the dream. Or perhaps she had drowned?

I held her tightly. She sobbed and moaned and soon the horrible cycle repeated itself once more. Fatigue—short sleep—screaming. And the fear of having to die.

At some point, she sent me away and only allowed a servant to stay in the room with her. In a harsh voice, she implored me not to sacrifice my sleep as well.

So I pulled away, helpless, despondent, but hearing her cries again several more times during the night—across the house—while I tossed and turned in despair on my own bed.

The next morning, I was faced with a difficult—and momentous—decision. For days I had been sitting on tenterhooks over it, but now felt I really couldn't put it off any longer.

I had arranged a meeting with a merchant who came from the far north, and whose acquaintance I had only recently made on one of his visits to the Carnuntum market.

The man, who called himself Saturnius even though he was certainly not a Roman, had amber for sale: the gold of the north, and pieces of choice quality. He described to me the rich deposits in his homeland that were in his possession, which he wanted to turn into money, and I was interested in buying the coveted gems from him. They were the perfect commodity—small, nonperishable, but at the same time very valuable.

The Romans loved amber, had jewelry, small vessels and all sorts of ornaments made from it, and they were willing to spend handsome sums for this luxury.

So I agreed with Saturnius that I would visit him in his homeland as soon as possible, to see his sites for myself, and if those looked promising I wanted to enter into a longer-term trading partnership with the man.

A week or two ago, I ought to have already started this journey in order to be at the destination at the agreed-upon time. But it was out of the question to leave Alma alone in her present condition. Well, she would not have really been on her own, or even lonely in my absence. She had friends who lovingly cared for her—but still, the long journey to the north was really the last thing I felt like doing at present, given her state.

That morning, as I was about to send a messenger to cancel the trip with the new business partner, or at least to postpone it for a few weeks until my affairs were in better order, Layla jumped out of her carriage on the front lawn of my house. Again, Telephus was her companion.

He greeted me, and then disappeared into the servants' quarters of my estate, presumably to have a second morning meal. He ate happily and abundantly, which was perhaps necessary to keep his form from his more active days as a gladiator, and the bodily strength that came with it.

Layla immediately saw that something was bothering me, and I only had to mention the "amber journey" in monosyllables and she immediately knew what my problem was. I had not concealed from her in the last weeks that I should actually have set out long ago.

Instead of advising me to postpone, as I would have expected, she came to me with an unexpected suggestion.

"I think you should ask Nemesis and Optimus to make the trip on your behalf," she said as she escorted me into the house.

"I really couldn't expect them to," I objected. "Don't you realize that this trip will take several months?"

"Yes, of course," Layla said, "but you know, both Nemesis and Optimus feel grateful to you. They both enjoy your hospitality, there's no doubt about that, but the sedentary life, the idleness, doesn't agree with either of them—neither the fearless gladiatrix, nor the brave veteran of the Legion. You would be doing them both a favor by offering them an adventure."

"But—" I began, but stalled.

I could not think of a real objection. The two of them might be inexperienced when it came to trading in general, or amber in particular—but they would be able to ascertain when on the spot the size of the stockpiles, the quality of the sites, and the respectability of my potential new trading partner, and to buy a small consignment for me. I wasn't risking a fortune by doing so.

I myself could always deepen the business relationship with the merchant at a later time, if this really seemed worthwhile. And I knew that Layla was right about the two of them staying as guests in my house.

Nemesis had given up her fights in the arena for the time being—because Optimus had literally begged her to do so. He didn't want to see the woman he had given his heart to spill her blood in those perilous sands. And this danger was a constant companion for a gladiatrix. Not many fighters retire.

But just sitting around being a good housewife and enjoying the comforts of a sedentary life—the brave Amazon would probably never be able to make her peace with that.

Optimus himself was a man who loved adventure and danger. So a journey into little known territory, full of hardships and predictable—or at least manageable—risks, was perhaps just the thing for the two of them.

"I will make a proposition to Nemesis and Optimus," I said to Layla.

She nodded with a smile, and I suspected that she had spoken to them already.

However, when I asked my friends later if they wanted to visit Saturnius on my behalf, they agreed without even asking for time to think. Indeed, it seemed that both the gladiatrix and the veteran of the legion were only too willing to explore the far north.

"An adventure in the land of the barbarians," Optimus joked, while Nemesis made Layla promise not to leave Alma's side while she was away.

Which meant that Layla would temporarily move into her former room in my house, while I made the necessary preparations for Nemesis and Optimus to start their "amber journey" that same day.

The two brave fighters refused to take a large escort with them. After all, on the way there they would only be carrying a few small gifts and trinkets that I'd given them for my potential new trading partner, and on the way back they would also only be carrying an inconsequential amount of amber—a trial delivery, so to speak.

Also, Nemesis reminded me that she and Optimus were exceedingly defensible travelers, as she put it. Of course I couldn't disagree with that.

At lunchtime that same day, as we all sat together over a meal of cheese, bread, and cold roast lamb in one of my dining rooms, Layla told me about her visit yesterday to the house of Latobios.

"I managed to speak to the boy Timor, whom Olivia said was Chelion's lover," she began. "He is fifteen years old, from Dalmatia, and has been serving in the house of Latobios for barely three years. The charioteer bought him while he was still in Rome, and then took him—with most of his household—with him when he moved to Vindobona."

"Is Timor then a beautiful youth, perfect for the pleasures of love?" I speculated.

Layla furrowed her brow. "Not really. He is of a most friendly nature, but truly not of a pleasing appearance. And when I asked him if he had been Chelion's lover, he actually denied it. He does not want to be known as the dead man's boy toy, neither for money, nor of his own free will. He seemed to be honestly astonished when I asked him about it."

"Hmm, how strange. I guess Olivia was perhaps mistaken then? Or, do you think there's a chance the boy is lying? Did he have anything to report regarding the scribe's death, then?"

"Unfortunately, no. He swore to me that Chelion had had no enemies—and he seemed very sincere to me, by the way. I don't think he was trying to fool me. But still..."

"Yes?" I encouraged her.

She shrugged and took a sip of wine from her cup. "It seemed to me that he knew more than he was willing to tell me. But perhaps I am mistaken; the good Timor may simply not be an eloquent fellow."

XII

The very next afternoon a messenger from Luscinia arrived, bringing us the promised blanket. It was made from the skin of a donkey—which is known to help against fear and terror, so much so that even small children are often covered with them.

The witch's special blanket had writing on the back, that is, on the tanned hide inside, with some short texts and strange symbols. The words were written in a script that I could not decipher, and I speculated the ink that had probably been used was blood.

Hopefully that of a sacrificial animal, not an innocent infant, the thought went through my mind. I brought the blanket immediately to Alma, and hoped that her suffering might be alleviated thereby.

What can I say—less than an hour later, her terrified screams rang through my house again. And over the next few days, it didn't get any better. Rather, it seemed to get worse.

I was being forced to watch my beloved as she turned more and more into a shadow. She had already lost quite a bit of weight, because she hardly liked to eat anything anymore, and now her face looked as sunken as that of a woman doomed to die.

Telephus, on the other hand, was enthusiastic about the eye elixir that Luscinia had sold to him. He was applying it exactly according to her instructions—in the morning at sunrise, and then in the evening at sunset—and swore to me that it was working true miracles.

"My eyes feel like new, Thanar! The world has regained its sharpness! And color, too!"

His joy comforted Alma a little, and the obvious effectiveness of the eye elixir finally made us decide to take Alma herself to Luscinia. After all, the witch had suggested a personal consultation in case the amulet and the blanket were not enough to free Alma from the horrific nightmares. And obviously Luscinia knew her craft; Telephus was singing her highest praises with a vigor I'd not seen in a long time. So Layla, Telephus, and I loaded Alma into my most comfortable carriage and headed for the patch of woods south of town that served as Luscinia's encampment.

The witch seemed a little surprised to see us again. She had probably trusted that her amulet and the donkey pelt would be enough to heal Alma, but when we all sat down together in the already familiar place under the oak tree, and she took a closer look at my beloved, her brow furrowed.

"Unbelievable," she muttered to herself as her blue-gray eyes bored into Alma's body like daggers. She seemed to see something otherworldly that was hidden from us mere mortals.

Finally, she stroked Alma's shoulders with her hands, and also touched her face with her fingertips, but in the end she pulled them away as though she had burned herself on my beloved's skin.

"I've never encountered anything like it," she said, again more to herself than to us.

"What?" I asked impatiently. "What do you see?"

She turned her head to me, and looked at me as if she had just awoken from a deep trance.

Finally, she addressed Alma: "You are possessed, you poor woman! And by that, I mean by *several* spirits of the dead. They cling to you, suck the life out of you—and it is they who are giving you the terrible nightmares. Tell me, do you see people dying in the worst of your dreams?"

Alma, leaning against my shoulder and taking heaving breaths, shook her head barely noticeably. "I don't see anyone die—I die myself, in a hundred different ways. By fire, by the sword, on the cross, on the stake, in the sands of the arena...."

"All deaths intended for villains," said Luscinia. "It seems to me it's a whole gang of criminals haunting you, clinging on to you rather than entering the realm of the dead. It's possibly because they fear the punishments that await them there."

She looked at Alma again, in that same penetrating way I have already described. "And it seems to me that they are also out for revenge," she added then.

Layla, who was sitting to the left of Alma, Telephus, who had taken a seat behind us, and I all exchanged silent glances. Alma was so weak that she just stared wordlessly at Luscinia, and didn't seem to understand what the witch was saying.

The rest of us immediately deduced which villains we were talking about here: the members of the band of robbers who had kidnapped Alma. They had been criminals of the worst sort, and in the end they had all, including their leader, been staked out along the Limes Road. Their bones had later been dumped—after being pecked clean by carrion birds—in the waters of the Danubius. If these despicable scoundrels still pursued Alma from beyond the grave....

By all the gods, the very idea made my blood run cold!

"What can you do?" I turned imploringly to Luscinia. "Can you drive those ghosts away? Will you save Alma from them?" I pleaded.

The witch nodded slowly. "I suppose I can, but it will not be easy. Alma must descend to the Underworld, where these criminals belong, to dispose of their lost souls. And these spirits won't let go of her willingly, I'm afraid."

She grabbed Alma's hand. "You must stay with me, and I will prepare the necessary ritual for you. I won't lie to you, it will be hard. You will suffer pain, and great anxiety. And you must muster all your strength if you want to be free in the end. If you don't, the villains will soon prevail, and drag you into the darkest depths of Hades where no one can save you, not even the most powerful of my kind."

The words seemed to rouse Alma. She disengaged herself from my shoulder, sat up straight, and nodded bravely. "I will do as you advise, Luscinia," she said solemnly. "I will be strong."

It broke my heart to hear how weak her voice sounded despite these brave words.

I put my arm around her. "I will stand by you, my dear," I vowed to her. "If you must descend into the Underworld, I will accompany you. I will not leave your side."

Alma gave me a tender smile, but Luscinia shook her head. "It doesn't work that way, Thanar, I'm sorry," she said. "She's the only one I can take to the Underworld, because that's hard enough. It's like...."

She hesitated, then fixed her piercing gaze on me and added, "It's like a new birth. Alma has to leave everything behind, everything and everyone dear to her—that's the only way she can get rid of these parasites, too."

I wanted to protest, but Alma reached for my hand and squeezed it gently. "I feel I'm in good hands with Luscinia," she assured me. She gave the witch a smile. "I trust her."

Luscinia acknowledged the words with a barely perceptible nod.

Then she turned to me again. "You can bring her a change of clothes, Thanar, but nothing else, I'm afraid. That is all she can take with her, to the place I will lead her. I will provide warm blankets for her. She shall not be cold, at least not in the body."

My hackles stood on end at the witch's words.

A journey to the Underworld. Few mortals had ever taken this path—and even fewer had returned to tell the tale. There were some legendary, not to say infamous, entrances to the world of the dead in the Empire: the Necromanteion in Greece, for example, where one could also consult the famous Oracle of the Dead, or the Plutonium in Asia Minor, dedicated to the god of the Underworld....

In addition, a powerful witch was supposedly able to gain entry through crypts, deep well shafts, caves, or tombs. Or via fresh, bloody battlefields.

The descent into Hades was perhaps not the problem at all, if one knew what one was doing and mastered the right rituals to gain entrance. The return was much more of a challenge.

Who would want to descend voluntarily into the realm of Pluto, only to possibly never find the way home again? Orpheus, the famous singer and poet, had tried it to bring his

Eurydice back to life. With his song and his lyre, he'd even succeeded in appeasing the hellhound Cerberus, but later, on the way back to the world of the living, even this great hero had failed miserably.

Did this Luscinia really know what she was doing? Was she, in the end, a mad murderer who wanted to sacrifice my beloved Alma to her even darker gods in some evil ritual? Her donkey pelt and amulet had already failed....

I caught a glance from Layla. She said nothing, but she nodded at me. Apparently she, too, trusted the witch, in the same way Alma did. I could only hope and pray that the famous female intuition, which remained a mystery to me, was not mistaken this one time.

I turned back to Luscinia. "I'll have the best food brought for Alma," I began. "And also—"

Luscinia raised her hands defensively. "No food, Thanar. And to drink, only water and consecrated wine, which I will provide for her. She will fast while we prepare her and purify her soul for the ritual. Nor will she eat any human food on her way to the Underworld."

A groan escaped me. Alma was already so emaciated! And now she was supposed to fast, too? For several days, from what Luscinia had been saying?

I swallowed and moistened my parched lips with my tongue. I tried hard not to let my renewed doubt, and the despair that gripped me, show.

We have no other choice, I said quietly to myself.

I believed the witch's observation, that Alma was doomed to die if she did not find help quickly. I had been watching her rapid deterioration at close range for the last few weeks.

Alma breathed a passionate kiss against my lips in farewell, while I desperately pressed her body—so bony now, and thin—against mine.

When Telephus, Layla and I had started on our way home in our carriage, and the witch's camp was already out of sight, Telephus had our coachman stop.

Nimbly he jumped out of the car.

"I'm going to stay here," he explained to us. "Near Luscinia's camp, so I can keep an eye on her—and on Alma. Unseen of course, so don't worry, Thanar. I know how to hide."

"Thank you," was all I could get out. The man was truly a brave and faithful friend, and I trusted his judgment.

"Send me a helper with supplies, Thanar," he asked. "A fellow with a swift steed whom I can send to you as a messenger should anything unexpected happen here. I will, of course, intervene if danger threatens Alma, but you shall know of it as soon as possible."

"And I will rush over immediately when you call me!" I vowed to my friend.

XIII

Layla asked me to make a detour on the way home so that she could stop by the baker, Dexippa. We had nothing to show for our investigation, no new findings concerning the death of her son, Chelion—but Layla at least wanted to assure her client that we hadn't given up on the matter. She really took her role as a Detector very seriously.

So we took a shortcut that would take us around the considerable traffic of the civilian city, and on a direct route to the camp suburb. It was no more than a bumpy dirt road—a route I would never have expected Alma to take in her condition, and which I would have liked to have spared Layla from, too, if the suggestion to take this pathway had not come from her.

It was already dawn when we left the forest behind us and approached the camp suburb. We passed the first graves lining the street—rather modest tombs, because the rich of the city made a point of finding their final resting place on the main arteries and in the immediate vicinity of the city.

Layla suddenly let out a sound of astonishment.

"Stop! Stop the carriage!" she shouted to the driver. The next moment she had jumped out of the car as nimbly as a cat. She turned to me. "Didn't you see her? That figure—in cloak and hood? She was just tampering with that grave over there!"

I also jumped out of our car, and followed Layla at a run. She was already heading for the grave in question.

I had not seen anything at all, especially not a dark figure. *Is my eyesight slowly going downhill, too?* I asked myself, seized by a sudden worry. Or was Layla seeing wraiths? It would not have been too surprising after our visit to Luscinia.

In any case, she walked fearlessly and without hesitation toward the grave she had pointed out. It was a shabby little tomb, probably not maintained for many years.

This did not necessarily mean that the family that owned the gravesite neglected their ancestors. There were many reasons why graves fell into disrepair, sometimes simply because the last of the clan had made the journey across the river of the dead, and there was no one left to take care of the tomb.

However, it was not this grave that was Layla's goal. She looked at the walls of the tomb, the barely legible inscription, and the rather bumbling stonework at the base, but finally she knelt down at the head of the grave that was located next to this shabby monument. It was a freshly-dug burial, poor, the earth still dark and damp. Only a tiny stone watched over the dead.

"Look," Layla said as she pointed to a spot between the earth and the stone with her hand. "Someone has been digging here. And it was after the dead man was interred."

I squinted with my eyes. Twilight was advancing rapidly, and we had not taken a lamp from the car.

To my horror, Layla drove her bare hands into the earth and began digging up the grave like a woman possessed.

"Don't!" I cried, "what are you doing?"

I wanted to grab her by the shoulders to put a stop to her insane actions, but at that moment she found what she had apparently been looking for.

She pointed into the hole she had created in the earth with her hands. I blinked, because I could not believe my eyes.

A slashed frog lay buried here, and there, where its innards should have been, was a paper-thin, rolled-up lead tablet. It was stained all over with the poor animal's blood and yet shimmered silvery-gray in the moonlight.

"A *defixio*," I cried, startled. "Don't touch it!"

I already saw a dark vision before me, in which Layla—by touching the tablet—also caught a deadly shadow, similar to what had happened to Alma after the execution of the band of robbers.

A lead tablet, hidden in a fresh grave, stained with the blood of an animal that was to be attributed to the goddess Hekate ... this could only be a curse. The Latin name defixio—which meant to *fasten* or *pierce*—came from the fact that these small lead tablets were often pierced by a nail or something similar.

In this way, one hoped to magically inflict pain and damage on the hated person to whom the imprecation was directed, and to give the spell the necessary emphasis. The tablet that Layla had dug up had also been impaled in this way.

As I looked around to see if there was any hint of the figure in the cloak and hood, something else occurred to me: we were at a crossroads, even if the road leading off from here was a still more insignificant dirt road than the bumpy track we were on. But it was a crossroads, and that was all that mattered. It was therefore one of those places where Hekate, the dark goddess of sorcerers and necromancers, was best invoked.

"The work of a witch!" I cried, and Layla nodded. Surely the shadow Layla claimed to have seen had buried the defixio in the grave. Fresh burial sites were the ideal place to invoke dark gods or demons from the Underworld. Or one used the aforementioned well shafts, battlefields, and other entrances to the Underworld to effectively place a defixio.

I was still holding Layla's arm to keep her away from the cursed tablet, but she resolutely broke away from me now, and got down on her knees.

Before I could stop her she had pulled the lead tablet from the frog's mutilated body. I felt the urge to vomit as she fearlessly unfolded the thin tablet and began to study the inscription.

"Nothing will happen to me, Thanar," she said in a calm voice. "But perhaps it's important to know what kind of curse this is. After all, we are dealing with a witch, who is said to have cast such dark spells."

My breath caught in my throat. Together with Layla, I bent over the tablet. It was full of symbols and covered with tiny characters that were barely decipherable.

By our combined forces, Layla and I were able to determine that it was a revenge spell. A murderer who had escaped unpunished for his crime was to be brought to justice by Mercury, Pluto and Hekate, as well as the Furies. It was quite usual with such spells to call upon as many gods as possible to make sure that at least one of them would actually intervene on behalf of the petitioner.

"The murderer of my beloved son Marcus shall be bound in shackles and suffer the most terrible tortures until his death," Layla read haltingly.

I could hardly see anything myself. The tiny letters blurred in the twilight before my eyes.

There followed a list of just about every abomination that could be inflicted on a murderer, and each of these extremely imaginative punishments was to end in death.

Just as one called several gods or other powers to one's aid in order to make the defixio effective, one also repeated over and over again in the incantation what one wanted to do to the hated enemy. One killed him therefore not only once, but to be on the safe side immediately in half a dozen ways.

That was the end of my knowledge about such tablets. I would never have thought of using such a defixio in my life.

"Marcus," Layla repeated when she had deciphered everything. "That was the name of Martianus's son, wasn't it? The little boy who died. Avernus, the medicus, spoke of him to Latobios the other night, and he advised him to take Martianus to Luscinia so that he could be cured of his delusion—do you remember?"

I had of course not forgotten that supper, or Avernus's report about the delusional centurion. But I didn't like what Layla was suggesting.

She looked at the tablet again. "According to Avernus, Martianus is haunted by this very notion: that his boy did not die a natural death, but was murdered. And this curse here proceeds from the same assumption. A boy named Marcus who was killed, and killed by a murderer who apparently got away with his crime."

"Marcus is a very common first name," I pointed out. "It could be another boy who died, and not the son of Martianus—and thus another father who commissioned this curse from a witch. Children die more often than adults, after all."

"But they don't get murdered every day," Layla said. "I don't really believe it's a coincidence, Thanar," she added with a serious expression. "In a city of millions like Rome, such a thing would certainly be possible, but in Vindobona? No...." She shook her head.

I didn't want to believe that Luscinia might be behind this heinous curse. Was this her way of curing Martianus of his insanity? By magically bringing the murderer of his son to justice with the help of a deadly curse and calling on dark gods?

Had the witch been the figure that Layla had seen disappear among the graves? Had Luscinia, after we'd left her in the forest, rushed to this lonely crossroads where there was a fresh burial? The perfect place to conceal a defixio tablet, but a lot of ground to cover....

I pulled the hideous artifact from Layla's hands and dropped it back into the earth.

More than one path might lead here from the forest. Luscinia could have overtaken us—and she could not have known that we would pass this specific crossroads. Had the gods, the ones who'd wanted us to act as Detectores, led us here at the right time?

But perhaps Sagana, the witch's assistant, had buried the curse here on behalf of her master.

For understandable reasons, the principal invokers of cruel curses, who wanted to hurt or even kill another person with them, remained anonymous on their tablets. And the witch who formulated the curse for them and buried it in the right place also took care not to leave anything behind that could lead back to her.

So we had nothing but the name of *Marcus,* and our knowledge that his father wanted revenge for the murder of the boy. In any case, the curse would have suited Martianus, and according to all that we knew he had come himself to Luscinia.

"We need to talk to Avernus," I said to Layla. "He'll be able to tell us if he actually brought Martianus to the witch...."

Layla nodded, barely noticeably.

We looked at each other and stood there for a moment, like Greek statues.

Then Layla got down on her knees again and pushed some soil over the tablet until it was no longer visible.

"If the boy really was murdered," she explained to me, "this curse should strike the murderer, I think. Cruel as it may be. To kill a child is probably the most heinous of all acts of blood."

XIV

The very next morning, I met with Layla again. This time I made my way to the legionary camp instead of expecting her at my house.

We had agreed the night before to have an urgent talk with Avernus in the camp hospital. If Luscinia was really behind the defixio tablet that had fallen into our hands as from the lap of the gods, she was a liar and worse. Then we would have to snatch Alma from the clutches of that witch before it was too late.

I had spent half the night sleepless on my bed, with the disgusting corpse of the dead frog before my eyes and in worry over Alma's fate.

Avernus seemed less than pleased with our visit. We had to ask our way until we found him in one of the storerooms of the camp hospital, where he seemed to be busy checking the stocks of various remedies.

It was only thanks to Layla's status in the legionary camp that we were able to reach the legion hospital in such a direct way and without having to face any questions from the guards.

But as I've said, the reception there was not very friendly. Avernus seemed to be very busy.

However, we were not deterred by this. I asked the medicus straightforwardly whether he—following the advice of his friend Latobios—had brought his patient Martianus to

Luscinia.

Instead of answering me, Avernus waved his arms wildly in front of my nose and rolled his eyes.

"Speak more quietly, I beg you! Must everyone here know what means I have resorted to? Yes, it is true that I rode with Martianus to the witch, as Latobios recommended. But I only wanted to help my patient! I have already told you how he is. And that I had no other advice."

"I know that," I said. "And far be it from me to criticize you. I—"

Avernus interrupted me: "If they found out about my deed here in the camp, I would be a dead man! Or at least I would lose my job. So I can only swear you—both of you—to secrecy. Not a word about this witch! To anyone!"

He looked around, as if the walls of the storage chamber had ears and eyes that sought to spy on his darkest secrets.

Then he added—in an exceedingly suspicious tone—"Why are you even interested in my patient? What do you care about Martianus's fate?"

I told the man the truth. I described Alma's sufferings to him, and that we had left her in the care of the witch.

Layla added, "Luscinia says only a certain ritual, which is very dangerous, can save Alma. That's why we wanted to find out how Martianus was doing after meeting with Luscinia, and that's all there is to it. It's only our concern for a friend that leads us to you."

Avernus nodded and his features brightened a little. He seemed to believe our story.

"I cannot speak for or against the witch," he said after clearing his throat. "I took Martianus to Sagana, the assistant, as Latobios had advised me. And she led us into the forest, south of the city, where the witch has her camp."

"We know the place," I said, "but please go on."

"Well, I didn't expect anything good from this sorceress," Avernus said. "I think I did make my point very clearly about all kinds of magic the other day, when we dined together at Latobios's. But Luscinia ... she's very different from what I imagined her to be. Competent, you know? Wise, I would almost say, and a good person. She seemed to really want to help Martianus."

I nodded. My impression of the witch had been similarly positive.

Had Luscinia blinded us all? Cunningly deceived and misled us with kind words, or even put us under her spell with her magic powers?

The medicus continued: "Martianus at first regarded the two women—first Sagana, then Luscinia—with suspicion, as is unfortunately the case with him lately towards everyone. But Luscinia succeeded after a short time in instilling confidence in him. Immediately, his reticence changed into the complete opposite; he suddenly seemed sure that Luscinia could help him, that she would be able to track down the murderer of his little Marcus with her psychic gifts."

"So did she succeed in this?" I asked.

Avernus twisted the corners of his mouth. "You could say so. She withdrew from us for a while, into one of her tents, where she gave herself up to an inner vision or something like that. And when she returned, she told Martianus the following: his son had not been the victim of a murder, but had been carried off by disease. A judgment that I share, by the way. I already mentioned that, didn't I? Luscinia's exact words were: 'You—or your son—may have incurred the wrath of the immortals, who took him away for the sake of it. But no mortal ever laid a hand on the boy, I assure you. He lost his life neither by poison, nor by magic, nor by any other weapon.'"

"And how did Martianus take this divination?" asked Layla.

The medic grimaced. "He didn't want to accept her conclusion! Even though Luscinia did her utmost to convince him, and patiently at that. Instead of finally accepting that the death of his boy could not be avenged and there was nothing left to do but grieve, he offered the witch a lot of money if she could use her magical powers to find the murderer and bring him to his just punishment. The villain should be cursed for 'all eternity,' Martianus demanded heatedly. But Luscinia stood by her verdict. And finally, she sent him away."

"Perhaps she did so only because Martianus came to her in your company," I said.

"Excuse me? What are you trying to say?"

"I mean that, in the presence of a military doctor, she might not have been willing to agree to the measures he asked her to take because they were—well, against the law. Perhaps Luscinia feared you might betray her if she were to serve your patient in this way. Is it not possible that he later rode out to her again, alone? And that on that occasion he offered her an even more generous sum, with which he finally changed her mind? Could it be that Martianus then commissioned a curse from Luscinia against the supposed murderer of his son?"

Avernus shook his head. "A *curse*, you say? I really can't

imagine that. This is not the sort of thing this woman would do. I can't say I have a high opinion of witches, but as I mentioned before, Luscinia seems like a decent person to me, one who wants to help and heal. She could have taken a lot of money from Martianus; the man is grieving and was willing to do anything. But she didn't go along with his demands, which I think is honorable, don't you? And she certainly did not behave that way merely because I was present. So if you mean to imply that she took any heinous measures on behalf of Martianus—"

He shook his head again. "No. I really can't imagine that. How do you even think of it?"

"As I said," I replied quickly, "we are only concerned about my companion, that's all. We want to make sure Luscinia doesn't have any, um, *dark side*."

Avernus eyed me cautiously; suspicion had returned to his gaze.

I concealed from him the finding of the defixio tablet. Perhaps there was indeed another father in Vindobona who had lost a son named Marcus and had enlisted the help of a witch—other than Luscinia?—in order to catch the murderer.

This could not be ruled out, no matter how modest our population might be compared to Rome. And it was certainly not my intention to slander Martianus, a respected centurion.

"Now, if you'll excuse me," Avernus said. "I have plenty of work to do. And—I implore you to keep this conversation and everything you know about Martianus and this witch to yourselves. No one in the legionary camp must know about it, you have to promise me that!"

We assured him of our full discretion, and then we left the legion hospital.

XV

In the afternoon of the same day, Layla and I drove back to the patch of woods where Luscinia had set up camp.

I had packed some of Alma's favorite clothes and a blanket made of fine spun wool, which I had given her as a gift some time ago, and which she had used almost every day since then. Even on warm days she used to wrap her feet in it, as she always felt cold.

Luscinia received us personally, and wanted to receive the items I had brought for Alma.

"Can't I give them to her myself?" I asked. "I'd like to see Alma. Is she all right?"

The smile with which the witch had greeted us died on her lips. "I'm sorry—no one can go to her now. We have already begun the ritual I described to you, and Alma is on her way to the realm of the dead."

What a horrible phrase! I couldn't help the cold shiver running down my neck at the witch's words.

"Where did you take her?" I pressed Luscinia further. "Where is the entrance to the Underworld? And is she at least comfortable on her way? Is there anything else you want us to bring her that she might need?"

I received only a shake of the head. "She is in the right place," she said simply, then looked me in the eyes with some scrutiny.

"You must trust me, Thanar," Luscinia said, "if you want me

to save your beloved."

I nodded uncertainly. Could I do that—trust her?

Layla tugged at the sleeve of my shirt. "Let's go, Thanar," she said.

Reluctantly, I said goodbye to the witch and followed Layla. She was right; there was nothing more we could do here. No one, least of all Alma, would be served if I kept questioning the decision we had made and drove myself mad with worry.

So we climbed back into the carriage and let the coachman drive the horses away. But we did not go very far—only far enough that we were out of sight and hearing of the witch's camp. There we stopped, as we were expected by my two men.

The first was the good Telephus; the second was a man named Nonius, who was one of my most capable slaves. I had sent him out in the morning to meet Telephus in the forest, as I had arranged with the former gladiator to remain here—to be my informer at Luscinia's camp.

I had given Nonius a fast mare with great stamina and supplies for a few days, so that Telephus and he were well provisioned. The two of them would now watch the witch's camp, and if anything should happen that needed my attention, Nonius would immediately ride to my house and inform me. So much for our plan, which at least partially alleviated my worries about Alma.

Telephus stepped in front of me to report about some observations he had made on the evening of the previous day. In his own words, he had sought a scouting post in the undergrowth very close to Luscinia's camp, where he could observe and eavesdrop on all the events surrounding the witch.

"Last night a doctor came by," he began, "from the legionary camp. The one who was a guest at the villa of Latobios the other day."

"You mean Avernus?" I asked.

"Yeah, right. That's the one."

I exchanged a look with Layla.

"And what did he want?" I asked, turning back to Telephus.

"Well, I think he had something of a romantic tryst with Luscinia. Anyway, the two of them sat together for a very long time, eating and drinking in high spirits, and seemed to enjoy each other's company very much, if you know what I mean."

I could not believe my ears.

"Avernus came alone?" asked Layla. "He was not accompanied by a legionary? Or should I say a centurion? You may know him. His name is Martianus...."

"Martianus? Hmm, yes, I know who he is. But Avernus traveled here alone."

"And did he talk to the witch about Martianus?" I interjected. "Could you even hear what they had to say to each other?"

"I was able to, for the most part anyway. As you know, my hearing works perfectly. And my eyes may soon be back, too."

With these words, he pulled the vial that Luscinia had given him out of the pouch on his belt. The one that was supposed to restore his sight.

He patted it tenderly, like a lover. "I swear by this stuff!" he said with fervor. "And by the witch, too. She is a true master—"

"Yes, all right," I interrupted him, perhaps a little too

briskly. I was heartily happy for him that Luscinia had helped him—but that didn't make me trust the witch unreservedly.

I longed to hold Alma in my arms, at least for a short while. Where was she right now? Not just in body, but in spirit? Was she all right? Or had she just come face to face with Hades, the god of the Underworld, and was scared to death?

Can one even be scared to death in the world of the dead, in the face of the god of the dead? popped into my head. Wasn't one practically a specter already, even if only temporarily?

Damn it, that did not make the slightest sense! I would lose my mind if I indulged in such thoughts!

"Keep reporting, Telephus," Layla's clear and calm voice brought me back down to earth.

Our capable spy didn't pause for very long. "So the doctor and the witch—they didn't talk about Martianus. Or about anyone else who was sick. It was more about the healing arts in general. The two of them spoke for hours about all sorts of herbs, their uses ... and then about spells. Luscinia gave the medicus quite a deep insight into her secrets, if you ask me. I found that rather unusual."

He faltered for a moment and ran his hand over his chin. "*Really* unusual. And then, and this seemed the most extraordinary thing, Avernus asked her for a special book."

"What kind of book?" I interjected.

I didn't know how to classify what Telephus was saying. Did it speak well for Luscinia? Was it evidence that she was basically an ordinary woman ... who simply had her eye on a man?

Admittedly a friendship between the witch and the medicus

could not very well be called average, if it even was one. Avernus had been very defensive about magic, or being in any way associated with the witch. At least, that's what he had claimed.

"What was the book the doctor asked about?" I repeated.

Telephus' eyes widened.

"A spell book," he whispered, as if the mere talk of such a text were altogether unseemly, if not dangerous. "Avernus said that he had heard of a unique book that was said to be in the possession of the witch. A book of spells and potions, which went back in a direct line—brace yourselves!—to the legendary Circe."

"You're not serious," Layla snapped.

I too thought I had misheard.

Circe? She was perhaps one of the most famous—or infamous, depending on how you looked at it—sorceresses who had ever lived. Many centuries had passed, no, almost a millennium.

Circe was said to have been of divine descent. Some thought she may have been a daughter of the nymph Perse and the sun god Helios, while others claimed that her mother was none other than the dark goddess Hekate.

The latter seemed much more appropriate to me, since both women—Circe and Hekate—were true masters of the magic arts. Circe had bewitched the companions of the legendary hero Odysseus and helped him to travel to the Underworld as Luscinia now had with Alma.

Since the time of the great Homer, Circe had captivated countless poets and thinkers. Virgil, Cicero, Ovid and many others had written about her and her magic.

"Luscinia claimed to Avernus that her family went back to a niece of Circe," Telephus said in an awed voice. "Can you imagine? Generations of witches, and each passing on her knowledge, expanding and deepening it...."

He twisted the vial of his eye elixir, which he still held in his hand, between his fingers and looked at it as if it were a true gift from the gods.

"A niece?" asked Layla. "Are you talking about Medea? She was Circe's niece, they say, and an equally infamous witch. She drove a chariot pulled by dragon serpents, and her spells were so powerful that she could even restore youth to an old man. She was also said to be a true master of poisons." Layla turned the corners of her mouth—more out of admiration than disgust, it seemed to me.

Telephus frowned. "Luscinia did not mention the name of this niece, I'm sorry."

"Never mind," Layla said, even though she looked a little disappointed. Then she went on, "Did Luscinia admit that this legendary spell book was in her possession?"

Telephus looked down. "I'm afraid I can't say that either. Because, you see, just at that moment Luscinia's old servant appeared and interrupted the conversation. Bedran is the fellow's name, and he has an almost dog-like devotion to his mistress. He is her cook, coachman, bodyguard, and only the gods know what else. He never seems to leave her side. Last night, when she began the conversation with the doctor, she sent him to fetch wood for the fire, and water from the river."

"You mean she wanted to keep him busy so she could be alone with the doctor?" asked Layla.

"That's what it looked like to me," Telephus confirmed.

"Although of course you'd need wood and water to set up camp here in the forest. Anyway, the old man eventually returned, and Luscinia probably couldn't think of anything new to occupy him with, so he settled down near where the witch was sitting with the medicus. It seemed to me that he was eyeing the doctor quite suspiciously, almost as though he were seized with jealousy, I would think. Whereupon Luscinia got up and led Avernus into one of the tents, claiming that she wanted to show him some of her herbal remedies, but I think she just wanted to get out of the old man's sight."

He shrugged his shoulders. "In any case, I crept as close as I could to the tent, but had to be careful so that this Bedran didn't see me. He has sharp senses for his age, I'll give him that. Maybe Luscinia used a spell to rejuvenate him? Just like that Medea you mentioned, Layla." He glanced at her, and it seemed to me that he was wondering if she didn't have magic powers herself. I would have said so without hesitation.

He continued, disappointment resonating in his voice: "In short, I couldn't sneak close enough to the tent to follow the further conversation of Luscinia and the medicus."

He fell silent for a moment, seemingly embarrassed by his failure, then asked, "Do you really think that Luscinia might possess such a book? A work that contains the secret spells Circe passed on to her niece, so long ago?"

"Certainly not impossible, I should think," Layla said. "Maybe not the original book, of course, for no papyrus could defy the ravages of time for so long. But possibly the copy of a copy of a copy...."

I agreed with her assessment with a brief nod.

"Good work, my friend," I finally said to Telephus—and was about to board my carriage again. But he held me back.

"Wait, that's not all I have to report, Thanar. Another guest—or rather customer—came to Luscinia this morning. Namely, Hersilia."

"The wife of Latobios?" I asked incredulously.

Telephus nodded. "She was in a pitiable condition. Burst into tears as soon as Luscinia received her, and could not be calmed for a long time, although the witch tried her best."

"What were they talking about?"

Once again, the former gladiator bowed his head in shame. "Unfortunately, I could not manage to get close to them this time either. Sagana had brought Hersilia here on a cart, and then unfortunately positioned herself so near to Luscinia that I couldn't sneak close enough to hear. I could only pick up a few words. I made out that Hersilia no longer wanted to live, that her existence no longer had any meaning, and that only one question occupied her, day in and day out."

"But you couldn't hear what it was all about?" I asked.

"Unfortunately, no," Telephus said contritely.

I patted the man on the shoulder. "Nevertheless, my friend, you have done an excellent job! Are you willing to hold your position here for longer?"

"Of course, Thanar. Until your Alma returns safely, I will watch over her here. No matter how long it may take—I promise."

I saw him once again twirling his elixir vial between his fingers. He almost seemed to enjoy the assignment and being allowed to linger near the witch, whom he must consider exceedingly powerful. Almost as if she herself were a daughter of Hekate, like the legendary Circe once was.

"I'll pay Hersilia another visit tomorrow," Layla said to me as we made our way home in the carriage. "Maybe I can find out what has upset her so much, why she wants to die—and what she desired for Luscinia to do."

XVI

Early the next day, my tireless spy Telephus sent me a mounted messenger posthaste. It was Nonius, the fellow whom I had placed at his disposal for this very purpose.

"I bring news, sir!" cried the youth, as he leaped nimbly from his saddle in the forecourt of my house. "Last night, Telephus and I were able to make another observation, of which I am to tell you."

I had a cool cup of wine brought to the lad for his dusty throat, and a bucket of water for the steed.

Nonius looked heated, and it seemed to me that he had ridden like a demon in his zeal. His face was flushed, and the poor mare was puffing and steaming as if she had had to contest a chariot race in the Circus Maximus.

How came I to this comparison? Well, as I was to immediately learn, the person whom Telephus and Nonius had observed in the witch's camp was none other than Smertius, the son of our famous charioteer Latobios. And he, in turn, made me think of the Circus.

"This is getting stranger and stranger!" I exclaimed when I heard Smertius's name. "First Avernus, then Hersilia, now her son ... just what is driving them all to Luscinia?"

"Smertius did not seek open conversation with the witch," Nonius told me. "Rather, he came secretly into the camp. Well, no, only near to it—he came riding up to it with Sagana!"

"With Sagana? The witch's helper?"

"Yes sir. I was able to observe this, fortunately, because Telephus had placed me near the road that leads to the camp from Vindobona, while he himself kept an eye on the actual camp. He is an excellent strategist, I think," he added in an admiring tone, "and a legend among the gladiators! What an honor to be allowed to spy with him!"

I had to smile at the fervent enthusiasm this young man was displaying.

"Keep talking," I urged him. "Sagana rode in with Smertius? Are you sure?"

The fellow nodded eagerly. "Smertius is known to me by sight. The son of his famous father! Oh, I wish I could attend a chariot race just once!"

Apparently, Nonius was not only an ardent follower of gladiator fights, but was also fascinated by racing.

He took his mission seriously, however, and remembered that he should report to me straight away. He added: "I know Sagana from the witch's camp. I swear to you, master, it was these two who approached the camp together: Sagana and Smertius. She was sitting in front of him on the horse. He held her close—I think not merely so that she might not fall off."

I found myself scratching my head. First Avernus and Luscinia, and now Smertius and Sagana? What mismatched couples! What would come next? Hersilia and Bedran, the old servant of the witch?

"Go on," I urged Nonius, "what happened then?"

He chattered blithely on. "Smertius and Sagana dismounted," he reported. "She walked the last bit to the camp and met up with Luscinia there. Telephus reported this to me later when he and I reunited."

"And what did Smertius do?" I asked. "You said that he didn't want to speak to the witch?"

"He was snooping around, sir—secretly, of course. While the two women spoke and then disappeared into one of the tents, he crept around the camp as if he were looking for something, it seemed to me. And immediately afterwards, he vanished into the forest. He was quite determined, I noticed, so I decided to follow him. I hope that was within the scope of your directives."

"Yes, I would say it was. Absolutely. And where was Smertius going?"

"He seemed to wander around a little aimlessly at first—again, as if he were looking for something. A specific place in this case, and eventually he found it I think. It was a small cave, inconspicuously located at the foot of a densely wooded hill. He looked around again, probably to make sure no one was following him. Then he disappeared into the cave."

"And you followed him inside?"

"No, sir," said Nonius in an uncertain voice. "Not this time. I—well, I thought he might discover me otherwise. After all, in a small grotto one has little chance of remaining unseen. So I lay in hiding outside and waited for him to return."

"I understand."

It seemed to me that my brave slave had avoided the inside of the cave for other reasons. Such places were notorious among the people: in the best case, they served a bear or highwaymen as a shelter, and in the worst one met with strange creatures, the kinds that avoided the light. Creatures of the darkness, or even from the very abyss of Hades. As I said, such places can be entrances to the world of the dead.

"How long did Smertius stay in the cave?" I questioned my slave.

"A very long time, sir," Nonius replied. "It seemed to me that a good hour passed. Only after that did he return. As far as I could see, he was unhurt. He returned to his horse, which he had tied to a tree, and then made his way back toward the city."

"I wonder if he found what he was looking for," I mused to myself. And what could he have been looking for anyway? Just what could the scholarly Smertius be doing in a cave, of all places?

"I'm afraid I don't know," Nonius said. "But he looked more disappointed than elated when he left the cave. So perhaps his efforts were in vain?"

I praised Nonius, gave him a few coins, and then sent him back to his observation post with Telephus.

I would have liked to talk to Layla about what this new observation of our spies might mean, but she had not shown up at my house today. Presumably she had gone to the house of Latobios, as she had planned, to talk with Hersilia there.

If Layla could figure out what Latobios's wife had wanted with the witch, would we also get an idea of why her son had been snooping around Luscinia's camp and inside that cave?

I hoped so.

XVII

The next morning I waited impatiently for Layla to come to me and tell me how her conversation with Hersilia had gone. She had not sent me a message, but I assumed that her first steps today would lead her to me.

Like a man driven, I walked up and down one of the arcades of my house. The peristyle courtyard, bordered by the columns of the arcade, was full of beautiful flowers and their fragrance enveloped me beguilingly. However this morning I struggled to bear the sensual pleasure. Yes, not even the blooming splendor of my garden could give me joy.

Without further ado, I had a horse saddled, and set off for the legionary camp.

I was granted entry at the gate, since after all I was known to be a friend of the legate—and on the street in front of the Legate's Palace I finally met Layla. She was occupied with a woman and her body slave, but fortunately they said goodbye when they saw me.

Probably because of my impatience, I had been wearing a somewhat grim face—and I was probably marked as a barbarian in the eyes of this lady anyway. She was expensively dressed, and, as I learned from Layla, was the wife of one of the tribunes. After Marcellus they were the highest-ranking men in the camp.

Layla looked around the street. There was little bustle that morning, yet she suggested going inside, which was just fine with me. There we would be undisturbed, I would not be stared at, and what we had to discuss would not filter into the wrong ears.

The Legate's Palace was located in the center of the legionary camp and was a magnificent villa with many suites of rooms, shaded porticoes, and flowering courtyards, and was full of the art and other treasures that Marcellus had collected.

We settled in a room where there were comfortable couches—with ornate bronze feet and soft upholstery—and one could look out into one of the courtyards. Marcellus, fortunately, had not yet returned from his trip to the western support camps. He certainly would not have approved of our current problem.

Layla didn't let me fidget for long, but immediately began to talk about her visit to Hersilia yesterday. Apparently it had not been a success.

"When I arrived at the house of Latobios, Hersilia had already gone out," she reported to me. "I decided to wait, but she did not return for a long time. However, I took advantage of the opportunity to speak once again with the slave, Olivia. Even though it was she who came rushing to me when she learned of my presence. She was exceedingly excited, for the boy Timor had unexpectedly left the house yesterday morning."

"Timor? Dead Chelion's boy toy?"

"Well if you remember, he vehemently denied being Chelion's lover," Layla said.

I brushed the remark aside with an impatient wave of my hand. "He may deny it, but that doesn't mean he's telling the truth, does it? And what do you mean he left the house? He hasn't escaped, has he?"

"No," Layla said, "he bought his freedom from his master."

"Hmm. Most unusual timing, I must say—or maybe it wasn't? Possibly the boy had saved up enough money for quite some time and was only staying in the house because of Chelion? To be near to him. And now that the latter is dead, there was nothing holding him there?"

"It's possible," Layla said, "but it seems unlikely to me that such a young slave would already have enough money to buy his way out. And Olivia assured me that he had never spoken of it—that is, of saving up for his release."

"Perhaps Chelion had paid him for his labors of love?" I suggested. "And Latobios probably agreed to the boy's request, to his desire to buy his freedom, didn't he? He let him go free, for whatever sum he might have asked for. Olivia knew nothing about that, I suppose?"

"No," Layla said, "she couldn't tell me the amount. I asked Latobios about it, though. Later at dinner, when Hersilia finally returned and I was allowed to be her guest, I approached him about Timor's ransom. I asked, as if casually, if the boy had had to raise much money. Latobios would not tell me the exact sum, but assured me that he had not asked the boy for a fortune."

"Then I really wonder why Chelion wasn't allowed to buy his freedom as well—doesn't that seem strange to you, too?"

"Yes, it does," Layla said, "but I haven't been able to find out anything new about that, I'm afraid."

She smoothed the fabric of her tunic, lost in thought—today she was wearing a scarlet robe that seemed to be on fire—then she added, "Olivia now thinks that Timor might have had something to do with Chelion's death. The boy left the house in a hurry, she said, and was driven by guilt in her opinion."

"That's pure speculation," I objected.

"Of course," Layla said. "I also asked her about whether perhaps Chelion had given the boy gifts of money."

"So?"

"It's possible," she said. "Chelion had probably received generous allowances from his master for his services. He was always well dressed, and often visited the taverns, Olivia stressed again.... She really seemed to be well informed about him and his ways. So acting on a hunch I exclaimed to her, as if off the top of my head, that Chelion must have meant a lot to her."

"It seems that way to me, too," I said.

"And we are right about that, because she suddenly burst into tears and confessed to me that she had been in love with Chelion for a very long time. But he did not want to know about it."

"Because he preferred Timor to her?"

"That's what it looks like, yes," she confirmed.

"Poor woman. That must have hurt her a lot."

A new thought popped into my head—which Layla, as usual, saw immediately. She raised her eyebrows and looked at me questioningly.

"What if Olivia is Chelion's killer?" I blurted out. "Disappointed love is, after all, one of the oldest motives for committing a crime of passion. If Olivia couldn't have her beloved, perhaps no one else should possess him either, in her eyes. Especially not an adolescent boy."

"Well, I don't know," Layla agreed, "Olivia doesn't strike me as a killer—"

But we both knew that such an impression could be deceiving. Very much so.

I dropped my new theory for the time being and asked Layla, "Did you hear anything new from Hersilia? You said she returned for dinner? Hopefully you had a chance to question her then."

"Unfortunately, no. When she returned home, she told me that she had been visiting a friend in the camp suburb, and chatted a bit about robes, jewelry, and the latest gossip from Rome. I hoped that over dinner—or afterwards—I could unobtrusively ask her my questions, such as why she had sought out Luscinia and what she wanted from the witch. But at dinner there was an éclat. Latobios had again invited our good medicus, Avernus, and Smertius was also present, but we all dined in almost complete silence. No one seemed to be in the mood for conversation, and so I could not unobtrusively address a word to Hersilia and satisfy my curiosity. Everything I said to her would have been heard by everyone, that's how quiet it was in the room. But then, just as dessert had been served, there was a sudden commotion outside the dining room. Voices were raised and then a man rushed into the room. The house slaves tried to stop him, and they stumbled or were dragged in with him, but they didn't really have any means of opposing him. The man, in fact, was Martianus the centurion. He was carrying his sword—and he was raging with fury."

"It is better not to stand in the way of an angry officer of the legions if you value your life," I said. "But what on earth had enraged him so? What did he want, invading Latobios's villa uninvited?" It surprised me to have not heard such gossip in the camp.

"I haven't found that out yet. We'll have to ask Avernus about it later. In any case, he stormed through like a berserker towards the couch on which Latobios was lying with Avernus, and he would probably have slashed the master of the house across the throat if a stout-hearted slave had not intervened at the very last moment. He brought an amphora down over the furious centurion's skull from behind, so that he collapsed unconscious in a heap, and Avernus had him tied up and took him to the camp hospital.

As you can probably imagine, the dinner was over. No one had any appetite for sweet treats or a few cups of wine afterwards. Latobios retired, attended by his son, and Hersilia also hurried to her chambers. I stayed with her for a short while to reassure her a little, but she was not in the right frame of mind for me to press her with questions. I then returned to the legionary camp and hurried to the hospital to wait for Avernus, who should have arrived with Martianus long ago. After all, the two of them had left the house of Latobios before me."

"Yet they didn't show up?"

"No. Although I waited for them for quite a while."

"Strange. Where could they have gone?"

"I'll check on Avernus later and hopefully find out," Layla said.

XVIII

I returned to my house, where I had other urgent business to attend to.

I received a shipment from distant Castra Regina and held meetings with business partners that I had been putting off for far too long, but in between I kept asking my servants if any messengers had arrived from Layla, or if perhaps Nonius had turned up after having been sent out by Telephus.

But no one had any news for me. It was not until the next evening that a mounted messenger from the legionary camp brought me a quickly scribbled letter from Layla.

Meet me at the House of Latobios as soon as you read this! There has been another death!

I had my horse saddled immediately.

Another death? Had the mad Martianus managed to gain access to the villa again? Had he plunged his sword into the master's chest this time?

Terrible images rose in my mind's eye as I raced my horse across the Danubius Bridge. I started to feel as though I were in a dark dream; a completely confused nightmare. I didn't even know why Martianus suddenly had developed such a hatred for the former charioteer.

Could it be that for some reason—completely unknown to me—he thought Latobios was the murderer of his little son, for whom he mourned so deeply? Had grief already clouded his mind to such an extent?

Or could there actually be a connection between the former racer and the centurion's boy? That seemed impossible to me.

In the charioteer's house, I found not only Layla waiting for me, but also the corpse of the late master of the house himself, Latobios! Just as I had feared.

But Latobios had not died by the sword. He had been found lifeless—though externally unharmed—in the villa's bathhouse, in one of the warm water pools.

Olivia, who received us, led us now to the dead man. Of course, he had already been taken out of the pool in the meantime and he was now laid out in the anteroom of the small spa.

Layla immediately set about inspecting the body. This filled Olivia with obvious distaste, but the slave did not dare to stop Layla's actions.

"Did they find him underwater?" I asked the slave, while Layla bent low over the dead man and smelled his lips. Even I felt a little sick at the sight, I must admit, although I'd known of Layla's passion for investigating crime for a long time now.

"Yes, sir," Olivia said in a quivering voice. "Do you think it was some dark spell that drowned him? Did he die by a curse like our poor Chelion did?"

She did not speak it aloud, but it was clear to me that when she said the words "dark spell" and "curse," she was thinking of the witch Luscinia, whom she seemed to fear and loathe more than ever. It didn't take much to gather she blamed her for the run of bad circumstances around Latobios's estate.

"Oh, our master should never have allowed the forces of evil to enter our house!" she cried in a tearful voice.

Next to her, Smertius and Hersilia were present, or rather: the son of the house was present, but seemed to be so deeply in shock that he only leaned powerlessly against one of the roof pillars of the bathhouse, not producing a word.

Hersilia seemed to have lost consciousness altogether. She was sitting on the marble bench that occupied the front of the room, and had to be supported by two slave girls in order not to fall over. Her eyes were closed, and her breathing was intermittent and irregular.

Olivia uttered a tortured wail. "We are all cursed! Who can save us now?"

Layla let go of Latobios's corpse, wrapped an arm around the trembling slave, and conjured up a glass vial from the pouch she always carried with her. She administered a few drops of the elixir it contained, and spoke soothing words to the woman.

"There, this will give you relief. You should lie down for a bit, Olivia."

I, on the other hand, turned to the new head of the house, Smertius. I asked him what Latobios had been doing in the hours leading up to his death. Where he was, with whom he had met, and whether Smertius had observed anything particularly unusual.

He had not been near his father, I eventually got out of him with some effort. But Latobios had not left the house, either.

Smertius told me the name of the body slave who had always stayed near his father, and then asked to be allowed to withdraw.

Of course I did not refuse him this request. How could I? After all he was now the master of the house, and I merely a guest. But he did do me the favor of sending for the body servant he had mentioned before leaving the spa with a swaying step.

Hersilia was also escorted to her chambers shortly thereafter by several slave girls, who had seemed to rush from all parts of the house.

Latobios's body slave, an elderly man named Ulixes with a double chin and a voluptuous midriff, appeared in the bathhouse moments later.

Layla knelt again next to the dead man, probably wanting to investigate further, but was within earshot and certainly did not miss a word of my questioning.

"Yes, I went to see my master several times during the day today," Ulixes stated. And no, Latobios had not received any visitors.

"The master spent the morning in the stables, as he often did," Ulixes said. "He had lunch with his son and the mistress, then—"

He hesitated. He seemed to have to think about the rest of the day first.

Finally he said, "I didn't see the master then for an hour or two. Maybe he was lying down. He did that occasionally. In any case, he retired to his chamber and did not want to be disturbed. Later he let me accompany him to the bathhouse, where I helped him undress and wash off before the bath."

"Was he alone?" I asked. "Or did someone in the family keep him company?"

"He was alone, sir. That is, only in my company."

The slave's eyes widened, probably fearing that I might reproach him in some way for the death of his master.

Which of course I did not.

"The master complained of nausea, I should perhaps mention," Ulixes continued. "He assumed that perhaps he may have eaten too richly at the midday meal, but felt that a warm bath would give him some relief."

"Nausea," I repeated. I directed the words to Layla, who had finally let go of the body and joined us.

"Do you think Latobios might have been poisoned?" I asked her.

"That's what it looks like, yes," came her reply. "His tongue is swollen, his lips are of an unnatural color. I can't tell what was administered to him, but in any case I don't think he was the victim of some damaging spell. It was clearly a deadly substance. Unfortunately there are a lot of possibilities there, so I can't say anything more specific."

The slave uttered a startled little cry. "Poison, you say? How vile!"

Layla nodded in agreement.

"But who would—who *could*—there was no stranger in the house!" stammered Ulixes. "Not all day long."

"Are you sure no one crept in?" I asked him. "Maybe the centurion who broke into the house the other night—the one who nearly disemboweled your master with his sword?"

"No, sir, certainly not! The villa is well secured. The possessed man may have gained entry that night by pretending to be a friend of Avernus, who was our guest—that's how he got into the house—and after that he simply pushed aside the slaves who led him towards the dining room, drew his sword, and charged into the room. But never would he have succeeded in penetrating unseen to our master and poisoning him, of that I am certain."

I nodded. To me, this idea also seemed quite far-fetched. Besides, an enraged centurion would not resort to an insidious poison to strike down an opponent, but rather thrust his sword into his enemy's chest, as he had already tried to do.

"Have you seen the boy Timor in the house again?" Layla said, turning to the man. "Today or maybe yesterday?"

"Timor, mistress?" The corpulent slave shook his head vigorously. "No, he has left us. And I don't think he'll be visiting us again anytime soon. He spoke about wanting to leave the province; his dream was to travel to warmer climes and find happiness there."

"Do you think Timor might have had something to do with the death of Latobios?" I asked Layla when we had left the charioteer's house. "And that he might have killed Chelion, his lover, first—and possibly stolen money from him to buy his freedom?" This idea had just popped into my head. "And now he has returned to poison his master as well? But what on earth could have driven him to do that?"

"All I know is that the boy clearly plays an important part in this strange drama," Layla said. "We need to find him, and talk to him."

"You're right. I'll see about tracking him down. He can't have gotten very far yet!"

After I had dropped Layla off at the legionary camp and

returned to my house, I sent two capable slaves on swift horses to search for Timor.

Presumably he had left the city in a southerly direction, as he was supposedly being drawn to warmer climes abroad. But he was on foot, or we at least thought he had no mount. And if he had bought one, it was certainly not an expensive horse that could take him far. He may have come into money, or perhaps even stolen it, but he certainly did not have a steed that was faster than any of those in my stable.

I instructed the two slaves I sent after him to ask for the boy at every roadhouse, and at every way station; then it was only a matter of time before they would pick him up, of that I was sure. Both were experienced men who had traveled far with my caravans in the past and had proven to be very reliable. They knew their way around the roads of our province to boot.

XIX

The next morning Layla and I went to see Avernus the doctor in the camp hospital. In the meantime he had returned from wherever he might have been the other night, when Layla had been waiting for him and the shackled Martianus.

We found Avernus in what served as a treatment room in the camp hospital. Several stone tables were to be found here, on which wounded or seriously ill legionaries could be laid out to be worked on with a scalpel or other even more fearsome instruments. I thought I could detect the smell of blood, although the room was not in use at the moment, and a slave was busy scrubbing the floor.

Avernus pointed his head in the man's direction, putting his finger to his lips, and then suggested that we talk in his room. He probably wanted to avoid being overheard by the slave—which was just fine with Layla and me.

The doctor's living quarters were located in a building immediately adjacent to the camp hospital. It was a modest space with a narrow bed, two chests, a table with two chairs, and a bench. On the other hand, the room could have been called luxurious when compared to the accommodations of ordinary soldiers. Legionary camps were far from luxury hostels.

Avernus pulled up a chair for himself and had Layla and me sit on the bench.

"Well, what is your desire?" he asked. His tone was polite,

but he clearly felt little inclination to have this conversation with us.

I took the floor, while Layla just watched the man silently—but all the more attentively.

"Your patient, Martianus," I began without mincing my words, "where did he go? Is he here in the camp hospital?"

The medic's eyes narrowed. "Why do you ask? Why are you interested in him?"

"Isn't it obvious? After the incident the other night at Latobios's house? He nearly disemboweled the man with his sword."

Avernus made a dismissive hand gesture. "He was beside himself with pain—his son's death still haunts him. Oh, what can I say, more than ever!"

"You had him fastened into shackles and indicated that you were going to bring him back here, to the camp hospital. But it seems to me you've changed your plans? He's not here, is he?"

Avernus hesitated for a moment. Then he lowered his head into his hands and moaned softly.

"With respect, I really don't know what business it is of yours, but I didn't actually bring him here. I took him to—a colleague, where I knew he would be safe. Should I have brought him here while on a rampage, wild with rage? It could mean the end of his career for the men to see him here in such a state. One does not tolerate madmen long in a legionary camp."

"What kind of colleague?" I asked.

Again the doctor hesitated. You really had to pull every single word out of the man. But he probably realized that he would not get rid of us until he had answered our questions.

"Well, you know her: Luscinia. I took Martianus to her camp, where he could calm down. And she promised to do her utmost to rid him of his delusion."

I had not expected this answer, even if it did not come as a surprise to me. I knew, thanks to my capable spies, that the doctor and the witch had become close. Two healers who wanted only the best for people?

"Martianus has remained tied up and is under guard, I assure you," Avernus quickly added. "So he can do no harm. Not to others, and not to himself."

"Well, are you entirely sure of that?" I returned. "Latobios, whose life he threatened, was murdered yesterday. Perhaps you haven't yet heard?"

The medicus was either an excellent actor—or my words hit him completely unprepared and with great force.

He jumped up from his chair. "What are you saying? Murdered?"

"It is the unfortunate truth. Latobios died yesterday, and from the looks of it he was probably poisoned. And since Martianus has already threatened his life once, I wonder how well he was guarded in the witch's camp and how tight his bonds were. Couldn't he have escaped her?"

"What? No! I would have known for sure!"

Avernus ruffled his black hair with both hands. Then he added: "You can rely on Luscinia. She is a decent—and very learned—woman. That evil should be said of her is pure slander!"

"It almost seems to me that you've taken her to your heart." The words escaped me impulsively.

The doctor frowned, but did not try to contradict me.

I exchanged a glance with Layla. Should we tell Avernus about the defixio tablet, and what we had discovered at the graves outside the city?

Could I seriously doubt any longer that Martianus was the commissioner of this murderous curse? And that Luscinia had made and buried the tablet for him, even if Avernus might think her a saint by now? After all, Martianus had consulted this witch and no other, so who else but she could be behind the heinous spell?

Layla seemed to guess what I was thinking. She nodded at me silently, but with a knowing look.

So I came out with the story. I told Avernus everything we had observed that night at the fresh grave. I mentioned the cloaked figure Layla had seen, and described in detail our gruesome find in the slashed frog's body.

The medicus backed away, visibly gripped by disgust.

"How horrible!" he cried. "But you are surely mistaken, Thanar, as to the wielder of this curse. I would not put my hand in the fire as to whether Martianus would not resort to such a means; in the state he is in, he is probably capable of anything. So he may be the principal mover of this abomination. But that Luscinia should have cast the spell, that *she should have* made this tablet—I would never believe it! She has devoted herself to the good, and to the art of healing, how often do I have to say it? She would never be capable of something so monstrous."

The doctor spoke with great fervor, and I refrained from contradicting him, or even from starting another discussion about Luscinia's merits—and her possible dark side.

"Can you say why Martianus entered the house of Latobios and threatened him with his sword, then?" Layla now intervened in the conversation and steered it in a different direction.

Her facial expression was friendly, her voice soft. But her gaze, which she had been directing attentively at Avernus the whole time, now seemed to bore into his eyes.

He turned his head away, walked a few steps up and down the room like a trapped predator—but then he dropped back into the chair. Layla did not receive an answer to her question, however. Avernus just stared mesmerized at the wall of the room and seemed to sink into a daze.

Another question was burning on my tongue, concerning the doctor's conversation with Luscinia in the forest camp, which had been overheard by my faithful Telephus. In it there had been talk of a powerful magic book, which was supposed to go back to the legendary Circe. Such an artifact seemed to me to be not only highly dangerous, especially if it fell into the wrong hands, but certainly also highly sought after. People who craved power would certainly climb over heaps of dead bodies for it. So did this book have something to do with the terrible events—especially the murders—that were keeping Layla and me on our toes?

How could I ask Avernus about the book without revealing that his conversation with Luscinia had been overheard? It was out of the question to tell him about Telephus, my spy. As devoted as the medicus may have become to the witch, he might have exposed my faithful snoop.

I decided to rely on hearsay and gossip—that was always a good excuse, because everyone knew how casual rumors of this sort tend to spread among all walks of life, and how quickly even the seemingly biggest secrets could become common knowledge.

"It came to my ears that Luscinia is in possession of a very valuable book of spells," I said—as casually as I could. "Have you heard anything about that?"

The doctor eyed me critically, but to my relief did not ask how I had come to own this knowledge.

"I'd heard about it too," he said, but then he made a dismissive hand gesture. "The truth is, that book doesn't actually exist, Thanar. That is, it does, but only in Luscinia's mind. For you must know—and isn't this common knowledge?—that the very greatest magicians entrusted their knowledge only to their closest disciples, and that only from mouth to ear. Written texts may exist, but they do not contain the most powerful spells."

"I also heard that Luscinia's knowledge is said to go back to the legendary Circe," I continued carefully. "Or was it perhaps to some niece of hers?"

The doctor nodded. "I heard that, too, from Luscinia's own lips. And I have no reason to doubt it. We all have a family tree, Thanar, that goes back to the dawn of time. Otherwise we wouldn't be here, would we? We are the descendants of those families that did not die out—over the millennia."

"Yes, I know," I conceded, "but I can't name any of my ancestors further back than four or five generations, while Luscinia refers to what? Forty or more generations? Is it not a good thousand years since the divine Circe walked the earth?"

The doctor clicked his tongue. "Your calculation may be correct, Thanar, but great sorceresses cultivate ancestor worship to a different extent than we ordinary mortals. Can you not imagine that? They learn from their forebears and draw part of their power from them, and through their ability to see into the realm of the dead, even to walk there, are also able to commune with their ancestors. Aren't they?"

With the best will in the world, I had nothing to say in reply.

Avernus shrugged his shoulders, seemingly indifferent. "Luscinia spoke very openly to me about this matter. And I have, as I said, no reason to doubt her word. She admitted to me that she herself had started the rumor about the book of spells containing the knowledge of the divine Circe, and which is said to be in Luscinia's possession. She did it at the beginning of her career to increase her prestige, and to emphasize her abilities. Publicity, I suppose is what you may call it, or a folly of youth if you will. In the meantime, she no longer needs it—and she now regrets ever having spoken of this book, because people are always looking for it, wanting to get hold of it at any price. And some are not afraid to threaten Luscinia because of it."

"A really interesting story," Layla said. Her tone was once again as neutral as if she had merely been listening to an amusing little tale the doctor might have thought up on the spur of the moment.

"It seems to me that Luscinia really trusts you," I said to Avernus, "if she told you so readily that she merely made up the existence of this book."

"But the knowledge *is* in her possession, I told you that already!" the doctor returned, a little irritably. "What difference does it make if it was ever recorded on papyrus? Luscinia has great powers, and they may go back to Circe. It makes no difference to me. She is a kindred soul, and a healer as I am. And nothing else matters to me."

Well, I said to myself silently, *Luscinia is also a very attractive woman*—who had probably cast a spell over the doctor, and not only in her capacity as a healer, it seemed to me.

I didn't get a chance to address Avernus again, because suddenly voices were raised outside in the corridor leading across to the camp hospital. A commotion, here in the legionary camp?

Avernus and I jumped to our feet at the same time, and rushed to the door. Layla followed behind us.

Outside in the corridor stood a young medic who, like Avernus, served in the camp hospital. Waving his arms, and in a desperate voice, he was trying to keep a man at a distance who had grabbed him by the shoulders and was yelling at him.

In the man I recognized Gorgonius, the optio we had met at the inn where Sagana had stayed. There we'd overheard those disgusting words that he had addressed to the witch's assistant. Gorgonius had demanded that a woman—not specifically named—suffer the most unspeakable pain.

Now he shook the young medic he had grabbed and

shouted, "You must come with me. My wife is seriously ill, she needs help! At once!"

"But you know that we are only here for members of the Legion—" That was as far as the young medic got. He was staring at the raging optio as if he feared for his life.

Avernus courageously rushed to help his colleague. He ran up to Gorgonius, raised his hands placatingly, and first tried to calm the man down.

He succeeded in freeing the young medic from the clutches of the enraged optio. But this did not mean that was completely pacified, either.

"One of you must come with me. Quickly," he demanded again. "My beloved Amalia needs a proper doctor. Not some quack from the suburbs! Otherwise she will die—I implore you!"

The objection that the young medicus had raised, or rather tried to raise, was valid. Only the members of the legion should benefit from the treatments of the camp doctors.

But this regulation was sometimes overlooked, especially when it came to the family of a higher-ranking legionary. It was similar to the law that forbade soldiers to marry; many a legionary had a wife and children in the suburbs, and I had been able to observe on one or two occasions that a camp doctor had gone in and out of their homes.

The young medicus gave Avernus a questioning look, and the latter nodded to him after a moment's hesitation. "Go with Gorgonius," he said. "I'll take over for you at the hospital in the meantime. After all, we're not exactly swamped at the moment."

"Thank you," Gorgonius managed to grind out. The next

moment he had already grabbed the young medic by the arm again and pulled him away with him.

I did not get a chance to talk with Layla in peace about what the appearance of Gorgonius might mean. I had planned to return to my house with her and discuss everything that was going through my mind there, as an ever-increasing abundance of thoughts now occupied me, and threatened to throw me into confusion.

But we had hardly passed the gate of the legionary camp and were heading for the Danubius Bridge when one of my slaves came galloping towards us from the other bank. The short respite I thought I deserved was not to be granted to me.

"Telephus is waiting for you in your house, sir," the man called out to me as soon as he reached us.

His horse even threw him out of the saddle by a hair because he had reined it in so abruptly next to our wagon. Our draft horses shied away; the coachman uttered a curse, but fortunately did not lose control. The messenger managed to stay on the back of his horse with an effort.

When he had finally brought his steed to a halt, he called out breathlessly to me, "Telephus has been looking for you for a while, sir. We have already sent out several horsemen to find you. A messenger to the house of Latobios, where we thought you were—and I myself was about to go to the legionary camp."

Where I often stay, I thought to myself silently.

"Good man," I praised him. "Now you've found me."

I instructed our coachman to take us home as quickly as possible, and the rider escorted us.

I was eager to know what Telephus had to tell me. If he had come himself instead of sending Nonius, his helper, what he had to say must be especially important.

My eager spy was already waiting for me somewhat impatiently in the atrium of my house. Layla and I led him into our secluded courtyard, which I described at the beginning of this chronicle, and then waited eagerly to hear what he had to say.

First of all, his words were disappointing to me.

"The other night Avernus came riding late into the witch's camp," he reported. "And he had Martianus in his power, who was bound and roaring as if out of his mind."

Of this I already knew, but I did well not to interrupt Telephus' flow of speech. What followed now put the doctor's report, which I had just learned myself, in a completely new light.

"The witch managed to pour some potion into the raging centurion," Telephus continued. "Something to calm him down, I suppose. But it did not really succeed; Martianus screamed and raved, spitting at the medicus' feet...."

"Not the nicest way to treat your doctor," I interjected.

"Well, he probably no longer sees Avernus as his doctor," Telephus replied seriously. "But rather as his mortal enemy!"

"Excuse me?" The words escaped me involuntarily. "Just because the man put him in shackles and prevented him from committing murder? Surely Martianus—even in his delusion—must realize that the doctor has only his best interests at heart."

Telephus shook his head. "A murder, you say? One that Martianus was going to commit and on someone other than the physician? For it seemed to me that all his thoughts and aspirations were only for the death of that very medicus. He cursed him most foully, and swore to him that he would not rest until he had avenged himself on him."

"Avenged? On Avernus?" I asked, not quite following.

"That's right—for the death of his son Marcus. I could quite clearly overhear him blaming Avernus."

"This is ... a new development," Layla said. Her voice sounded calm as ever, but even in her eyes I could now read some confusion.

"Keep talking, Telephus," was all I could produce.

And the former gladiator did not wait to be asked twice.

"It seems that Avernus had been acquainted with Martianus for some time," he said. "And when Martianus's son suddenly fell seriously ill, he was able to persuade the camp doctor to treat the boy."

So far, nothing unusual. Only today we had been able to observe how Gorgonius had stormed into the camp hospital with a very similar request.

"The boy Marcus lived under the supervision of a maid in the suburbs," Telephus continued. "Alone, and without any other siblings. His mother—Martianus's wife—had died at his birth. But this maid, I don't know her name, apparently took very good care of the little one so that he had never lacked anything, and he had also been spared from illness. At least, that's how Martianus told it. And then suddenly, out of the blue, this deadly disease. Avernus rushed to the boy's house ... but could do nothing more for him. At that time Martianus did not blame him for the boy's death, but now he seems to have changed his mind. In the witch's camp, he accused the doctor of killing Marcus—out of envy, because he himself had not been granted a son. And Martianus is now burning for a deadly revenge!"

"Unbelievable," I said. "I wonder what drove him to this? How did he come up with this insane idea so suddenly?"

"Unfortunately, we did not learn that," Telephus said with a contrite expression. "For a mishap occurred at that moment: Nonius stepped on a dry twig in our hiding place, from which we were listening and watching. It cracked terribly loudly, so that the witch and Avernus became aware of us. Martianus didn't, he had talked himself into such a rage that he probably wouldn't have noticed anything anymore. But it didn't help; we had to flee. We stormed through the forest, and Luscinia's servant, Bedran, pursued us like a bloodhound! I would never have believed the old boy to have such agility in the forest still, and such endurance! He couldn't catch either of us, but he chased Nonius for quite a long time—and probably would have chased him all the way to Rome, if he hadn't lost his trail in the end."

Telephus twisted his face into a wry smile. "It took me half an eternity to find Nonius again. We had stormed off in different directions, to shake off the old man. And Nonius, the wretch, injured himself in the escape. His leg is badly dislocated, perhaps even broken. In any case, his ankle looks like—"

He broke off and shook his head. "Well, anyway, I got him back to our hiding place with some difficulty, and splinted the ankle ... but long story short, you'll have to send a wagon, Thanar, to retrieve him. He can't walk on his own, at least for now."

"No problem, we can manage that," I said immediately. "But the witch ... what has she done with Martianus? Is he still with her in the camp?"

Telephus cast his eyes down guiltily as if he had incurred my great wrath. "I'm afraid I don't know. When I had taken care of Nonius and crept back to Luscinia's camp on quiet soles to peep again, I could discover neither her nor Martianus. And Avernus was no longer there either. Only old Bedran had returned from his hunt for us, and was sleeping near the fire. It was not until dawn that Luscinia returned—alone."

"Well, she must have Martianus hidden somewhere," I said.

Perhaps in that secret place to which she had also taken my Alma? Hadn't Nonius recently spoken of a cave to which he had tracked the snooping Smertius? Could this be the secret hiding place of the witch? Was Martianus now lying there bound and gagged, while Alma...?

How was she, my beloved? Was she well? I had the feeling that the ground was swaying beneath my feet as if I were not sitting safely in the courtyard of my house but on a ship that was plowing through a stormy sea.

"Avernus has not told us a word about these incidents in the witch's camp."—Layla brought me out of my gloomy meditation.

"That's true," I grumbled.

"Or of Martianus blaming him for the death of his son."

Telephus took the floor again: "I spent the last few days

taking care of Nonius, and always keeping an eye out for what the witch might be up to. As often as I looked for her in the camp, she was there. I also saw Sagana once, and two visitors, who were probably customers of the witch. Nothing out of the ordinary, so this morning I left Nonius alone and hurried here to your house, Thanar, to report to you. With your consent, I will return at once to my post and resume my observation. But will you give me a man to relieve Nonius? And another with a cart or wagon to recover him?"

"Sure!" I said. "But you'd better send two of my men into the forest. One instead of Nonius, and another to replace you. Choose them yourself; you will know who is best suited. For you I have another task—you said you knew Gorgonius, didn't you? That optio we met at Sagana's flophouse—at Rufius's roadhouse."

"Yes, Thanar. What about him?"

"I want you to seek him out. It's best you find him when he is away from the legionary camp. His wife lives in the suburbs, so he'll probably own or rent a house there. See if you can talk to him in private. And that you elicit from him what he actually commissioned from Luscinia: who it was he wanted to curse."

"The woman who should be in torturous pain, you mean?" asked Telephus. The words we had overheard in Rufius's rest house had apparently remained in his memory as well as mine.

I nodded. "Find out who she is! And whether Luscinia actually agreed to curse her."

"Sure, you can count on me," said Telephus.

He turned to go, but I still instructed him to fortify himself in the kitchen before his assignment, and to allow himself time to sleep.

"Your mission is not that urgent," I added. "Send only the men to Nonius, that he may find relief, and that the witch's camp be not long unobserved. But then allow yourself a well-deserved rest."

Telephus thanked me with a nod of his head, then disappeared.

Layla and I were left alone and—at least as far as I was concerned—more confused than ever. Was it in the nature of this case, because a witch was involved, that so many seemingly inexplicable circumstances were coming together? That more than one person seemed to have lost his mind, while others had even lost their lives?

It seemed to me that we were drowning in chaos, blood and madness wherever we turned. Was it even *one* case we were still working on? Or had there been several for a long time? Would we ever have an answer for the baker?

A good dozen questions plagued me. For example, had Martianus not intended to take the charioteer's life when he entered Latobios's house? Had he in fact followed Avernus and intended to kill *him*, because he thought he was the murderer of his son?

The two men—Latobios and the medicus—had been lying next to each other at the head of the table. Perhaps it had only looked to the witnesses of the scuffle as if Martianus's lust for murder had been directed at the master of the house.

And Avernus—could he still be trusted? He hadn't told us anything about Martianus calling him a murderer. But what did that mean? That he was guilty of the heinous child murder of which the centurion had accused him? I could not imagine that with the best will in the world.

"We have to get Alma back," I said, turning to Layla, my skull aching. "I can't leave her in the care of that Luscinia any longer. She's in mortal danger there; I just can't shake that thought!"

XXII

So Layla and I went to the witch's forest camp again. This time I demanded to see Alma emphatically—without immediately revealing that I also wanted to snatch her from the witch's clutches.

Luscinia was as unimpressed by my appearance as she had been the last time. She refused to even tell me Alma's whereabouts, let alone allow me to see her. And she uttered a warning: "I told you that she must make the journey to the Underworld to be healed. This is not a pleasure trip, but a ritual in which she walks between the living and the dead. If you take her out of the prescribed paths in the midst of this rite, it can have the most serious consequences for her. She could return to you in a worse state than she was in when you brought her to me and fall into a much deeper abyss in the future, from whence no one can bring her back. So think carefully about what you do, Thanar."

"Then you'll just have to stop the ritual, finish it faster than planned," I hurled at the witch.

Her faithful servant, old Bedran, who had been lurking in the background, now stepped forward. Or rather, he rushed between us and inflated his chest in front of me.

"You will not harass my mistress!" he shouted, glaring angrily. "I won't let you!"

Luscinia stepped up beside the old man and put her hand on his arm. "It's all right, Bedran. We'll all calm down now, shall we?"

Turning to me, she added, "What is it that has you in such turmoil, Thanar? Why do you fear for your beloved so? Did not you yourself give her into my care?"

I retreated a step backwards while the witch pushed her servant aside. I took a deep breath.

"Well," I finally said, "I saw you in a different light when I entrusted Alma to you. What I have learned about you in the meantime makes me doubt whether she is really in good hands with you. I'm only concerned about her well-being—for her safety."

"What happened to make you withdraw your trust in me?" the witch wanted to know. She gave me a brisk look, in which I detected there was also something like uncertainty. At least, that's what I thought I perceived.

"You still ask that?" I cried. "Disease and death are wherever you go. They pursue you—or is it not rather you who bring ruin upon men?"

Luscinia moaned softly. "Do you still believe the slanderers who think me capable of evil?"

My patience was wearing thin.

"Slanderers?" I repeated, upset. "It seems to me that the people who accuse you of evil speak the plain truth. Will you deny that you buried a defixio in a tomb for Martianus, the centurion? That you devised a curse to find the murderer of his son, torture him most cruelly, and finally kill him? And did you not cast an equally dark spell for Gorgonius, the optio, to punish some poor woman—his wife, perhaps, who was thereupon stricken with a cruel disease?"

I was talking myself increasingly into a rage, and I wasn't

finished yet.

"In the house of Latobios," I continued without catching my breath, "where you supposedly only healed a sick horse, two men have died in the meantime, one of them being the master of the house himself. All this ruin ... do you seriously want me to believe that you had nothing to do with it?"

The color drained from her cheeks as I threw these words at her. She took a step back in turn.

"Indeed I do," she said in a raspy voice. "Because it is the truth; I know nothing of these things."

Layla intervened. "The two curses, on behalf of Gorgonius and Martianus—you mean to say you didn't cast them?"

Luscinia nodded vigorously. "I swear to you. It is true that Martianus came to me hungry for revenge; the physician Avernus brought him here, hoping to cure him of his madness. I gave back to Martianus what the gods showed me in my scrying, that his son had not been murdered, but had been carried off by a disease. He, however, would not believe my words and left me in anger. And finally he directed his madness at Avernus himself. But I have had nothing to do with that, and I certainly did not bury a defixio for him. The man named Gorgonius is not known to me at all." She thrust her chin forward and looked challengingly first at Layla, then at me.

Again it was Layla who took the floor. I let her, because I felt nothing but wild anger pulsing in my veins, and would have liked to wring the neck of this witch—and liar! Layla probably saw the state I was in and quickly intervened before I could do anything to Luscinia.

"We found a defixio in a fresh grave not too far from here," she explained to the witch. "It was to curse the murderer of a boy named Marcus, and for the life of me I can't imagine that it was any other boy than the son of Martianus. And as for Gorgonius—Thanar, I, and another friend heard your assistant promise him a dark spell to inflict great pain on a woman—his wife, we now assume."

"What are you saying?" gasped Luscinia. "Sagana is supposed to have promised him that?"

"That's right," Layla confirmed. "We don't want to malign her, or even you," she added with a gentleness I would never have been capable of at that moment. "But we definitely heard those words. And we found this defixio—a lead tablet—in the bowels of a frog, buried in a fresh grave, just as Thanar has described it to you."

Layla furrowed her brow and seemed to be pursuing an idea in her own mind.

Then she added: "Could it be that Sagana wrote this defixio for Martianus? You sent him away, but she may have offered her services to him. Would she be able to cast a curse? I assume she is well trained in the witchcraft arts?"

"Indeed she is," Luscinia said slowly. Her bright eyes had narrowed into dark slits. "Sagana is my adept. I trust her, and I have taught her everything I know."

She raised her hands. "And, before you ask—yes, of course I know how to put a curse on a lead tablet. Even though I would never do such things, I am of course familiar with such rituals, and so is Sagana. As is probably every witch in the whole of the Empire."

She twisted the corners of her mouth, and suddenly spoke more to herself than to us. "Could it be that my student has betrayed me?" Her voice had died to a startled whisper. "Is that why all this evil gossip is haunting me? Even in other cities, before I came here to Vindobona? I always wondered why people said the worst abominations about me...."

"Perhaps for that very reason," Layla said, "because Sagana performed the dark spells that you had rejected. Greed for profit may have driven her to do so, or a desire to prove her own witchcraft power."

"I really can't imagine it," Luscinia said, but by now she sounded less than convinced by her own words.

"Sagana, then?" I turned impatiently to Layla. "Is she the one responsible for all the evil and ruin we have encountered? Is she not only the caster of deadly curses, but the murderer of Latobios and his slave Chelion? But what in the name of all the gods drove her to these deeds?"

Layla raised her eyebrows, but didn't give me an answer.

"Could it be that Sagana befriended Smertius, the son of Latobios?" She turned to Luscinia. "The two were seen coming together here to your camp. Sagana went to you while Smertius was out looking for something. And perhaps he found it ... in a cave that lies near here."

"Looking for something?" echoed Luscinia.

"Well, a powerful spell book, I think, said to be in your possession," Layla said.

Luscinia closed her eyes and moaned softly. "Not again...." came powerlessly, barely audibly from her lips.

Before I could ask the witch another question about the spell book, which according to Avernus existed only in her head, she deftly changed the subject.

"Sagana accompanied me to the villa of Latobios," she said,

"when I treated his horse. And I had the impression even then that young Smertius had his eye on her."

"And she on him?" I asked.

"I think so. I didn't pay any further attention to it. I had a life to save, even if it was only that of a horse. But afterwards, Sagana approached me about the family. Asked me questions—only harmless ones, I want to emphasize, and I told her not to get her hopes up. A woman of her status, and the son of a millionaire? Such a union would never have been agreed to by a man like Latobios."

"Was Sagana of the same opinion?" asked Layla.

A smile flitted across Luscinia's beautiful features. "Not at all. She said, 'We're witches, aren't we? We can accomplish anything we set our minds to'."

"Very confident, I must say," I muttered to myself.

At the same time, a thought crept through my mind: had Sagana coldly eliminated Latobios just so she could get her hands on his son—and heir? Had she used her witchcraft powers to murder the man, whether by one of the insidious poisons she was familiar with, or via a deadly curse? The method itself made no difference, after all.

Layla voiced the same thought as we left the witch's camp and headed back to Vindobona.

"If Luscinia speaks the truth," she said, "and I believe she does—Sagana may be behind the curses and the damaging spells. And she may have used her witchcraft powers not merely for pay from men like Martianus or Gorgonius, but also for her own interests ... to land herself a rich husband."

"Smertius," I said, and Layla nodded.

"But why did Chelion have to die, in addition to Latobios?" I asked. "How could he have stood in Sagana's way? A simple scribe?"

"What if he wasn't supposed to die at all?" mused Layla to herself. "Maybe Latobios was Sagana's chosen victim from the start, and his poor scribe merely ate or drank something that was actually meant for the master of the house? It is not impossible. Many a slave enjoys a treat left by his master—"

"We have to grab Sagana," I said. "And interrogate her!"

We had not found Sagana in Luscinia's camp, so we now made our way to Rufius's rest house, where she had previously taken up quarters. Dusk had long since fallen.

When we reached the inn, we were met by a servant who lit the way with a lantern. We hurried up the rotten stairs, and rushed into Sagana's chamber—but found it empty. The witch's assistant was not at home.

"Should we wait until she returns?" asked Layla.

"No, that could take too much time. She may be with a client or indulging in some evening pastime. I'll put Telephus onto her, first thing in the morning. I'll have him find her and bring her to us. She won't be able to resist him, despite all her witch's powers."

At that moment, I remembered that I had already entrusted the ex-gladiator with another task: namely to find Gorgonius, and to question him about his cruel curse on a woman, and discover just who it was—his wife?

So I had to send out another hunter to track down Sagana. But that should not be a problem; I would choose one of my men who would dare to take on this poisoner and dark sorceress. And once Sagana was in our hands, we would get everything out of her.

XXIII

Before I could put my plan into action the next day, indeed before I was even really awake, not only did Layla reappear in my house, but she did so with Telephus.

He proudly reported to me that he had succeeded in tracking down Gorgonius the night before.

"I met him where I thought he would be, rolling the dice," he confessed to me, managing to look rather guilty. He didn't say it—and I didn't probe—but I deduced two things from his words.

First, he did not mean the dice game as it was officially permitted, but spoke of that forbidden variant in which people played for sometimes very high stakes. Many a man indulged in this vice, even if it was punishable. I myself was fortunately not susceptible to this addiction.

Secondly, I concluded that Telephus was also a friend of the dice himself. Apparently he knew the right places, mostly the back rooms of certain pubs, not just by hearsay, but from his own experience.

Which really didn't bother me. I appreciated the Romans and their way of life; but that didn't mean I thought every one of their laws made sense. Why ban such a harmless game?

"Were you able to question Gorgonius?" I wanted to know. "About the curse he had commissioned?"

"Indeed I was," said Telephus. "He seems to have come to heartily regret the deed. At any rate, he assured me of this when I made him believe that he had been overheard talking to Sagana. He literally broke down, which I hadn't expected from a man like him. He confessed to me that the curse had been on his wife, whom he'd believed to be unfaithful. She then fell seriously ill, and it is only thanks to one of the doctors from the legionary camp that she is still among the living. Gorgonius saw himself—and the curse he had commissioned—as being responsible for her suffering, and now deeply regrets the act. He had wanted to punish her, not murder her, he assured me. Moreover, at the bedside, she seems to have succeeded in convincing him of her innocence. She had always been faithful to him—he is now convinced of that."

"Tell me," I asked impatiently, "who worked the curse for him? Was it Luscinia?"

Telephus shook his head. "No, Sagana took that on directly herself, he assured me. She told him Luscinia would not cast any damaging spells, but she herself was willing, for a handsome sum, to match his then fierce anger and curse the supposed infidelity. I cannot swear, however, as to whether he is telling the truth on this point. We should question Sagana about it."

"That's what we're going to do, my friend. That's exactly what we're going to do," I said.

The hot-headed optio had thus confirmed Luscinia's protestations of innocence without even knowing it. Sagana was the one we were looking for, and we would find her!

I immediately told Telephus to make his way to Rufius's rest house, and look for the dark sorceress there.

"Bring her to me," I said, "whether she likes it or not. Will

you succeed, my friend?"
"Certainly, don't worry," he replied laconically.

Layla and I had the horses hitched up to the carriage and set off for Latobios's villa. We planned to have a serious word with Smertius, although we could not simply have him dragged off to my house like Sagana to interrogate him.

"I can well imagine that he was after his father's life," I said to Layla as we passed the legionary camp. "It seemed to me he was overshadowed by the victorious, successful charioteer that was Latobios. And maybe he was lusting after his millions, too. Then Sagana came along, turned his head—and he had one more reason to get rid of the old man. Don't you think?"

"It's possible," Layla said. "I, too, had the impression that he was quite in his father's shadow. But I wonder if such an insecure youth as he would even be brave enough to commit murder? To even risk it?"

"Well, Sagana may have poisoned the old man. Or, at any rate, prepared the deadly elixir—and all Smertius had to do was mix it into his father's food or drink. That doesn't take the same courage as plunging a bare blade into a man's chest."

In the villa of Latobios—or should I already be saying in the villa of Smertius, for it now belonged to him—we were readily admitted by the gatekeeper and politely received by the house slaves.

We were offered hospitality and refreshments, but the young master was not present. He had gone out, we were told, to attend to his father's funeral preparations. It was to be a magnificent, even spectacular funeral procession that Vindobona would not soon forget. A banquet was planned, with gladiator fights, the full program. And of course, Latobios would be laid to rest in a magnificent tomb near the city, decorated with sculptures of his noble steeds.

We decided to wait. Eventually Smertius would return home—and he did, barely an hour after we'd entered the house.

The only problem was that a second man appeared outside the gate as soon as Smertius greeted us, one who would not have been denied entry to any house in the city. And one whose appearance—now of all times—neither Layla nor I had expected.

It was Marcellus, the legate of Vindobona and Layla's lover, who came riding into the forecourt of the villa with some legionaries in his retinue. He was sitting on a magnificent, fiery red stallion, and the animal was panting as if it was about to collapse under my friend at any moment.

Marcellus jumped out of the saddle, ignoring the young landlord who'd first received him, and immediately came up to Layla and me.

He greeted us with a cool expression and extremely curt phrases, and promptly demanded a conversation in private with Layla and myself. He left his soldiers in the square, sent Smertius into the house with an impatient gesture, as though he were also under his command, and then took the two of us aside.

"What's going on?" he cried in an excited whisper. "It has been brought to my attention that a witch is wreaking havoc in Vindobona. Is this true?"

I wanted to say something back, but he cut me off. With wild fire in his dark eyes, he turned to Layla. "I have also been told that my own mistress has been consorting with this witch. As well as my friend, the barbarian." The latter words were directed at me, and I too caught an angry glare from the legate.

"So I cut my journey short," he continued in the same angry tone, "to hurry back to Vindobona. A journey, I would like to emphasize, which I did not undertake for my own pleasure, but which was very important—not only for me personally, but also for the safety of our province. And you can think of nothing better than to get yourself talked about by indulging in black magic behind my back?"

"Let me explain, Marcellus," I took the floor without defending myself against the vituperation of being a barbarian. Now, tact would be required here. I didn't want Layla to get into serious trouble with her beloved because of our entanglement in all this.

At the same time, I wondered who might have informed Marcellus about what we were doing. Who had told him about the activities of his lover and his barbarian friend in Vindobona, while he was visiting the auxiliary camps?

But the answer may have truly just been idle gossip. Hearsay was omnipresent, and Layla in particular—as the legate's companion—was inevitably at the center of public attention.

An officer of the legionary camp might have thought it necessary to inform Marcellus of our unusual activities. Even if the legate was traveling, he was still in regular contact with Vindobona, and a mounted messenger could reach the camps in the west that Marcellus had visited within a day or two. Along the Limes Road there was a dense network of way stations where official envoys could always find fresh horses at their disposal.

So I refrained from asking Marcellus what exactly he had learned from whom. Instead, I began to describe to him the events of the last few days and how we'd come to be involved—in a highly summarized form. He had already known about Alma's suffering when he left, because she had been haunted by her hideous nightmares for weeks. So I only had to tell him about how we had learned about the spectacular healing powers of Luscinia and that, based on these reports, we decided to lead Alma to her.

"It was our last hope, Marcellus," I said to my friend, "and you can believe me that the decision to trust Luscinia was truly not an easy one. I have already regretted it more than once in the meantime—although now it seems again that the witch is indeed committed only to the good, for what it's worth."

The anger that had just blazed in Marcellus' eyes ebbed away. He was not inhuman. He knew what Alma meant to me—and if Layla had suffered similar torments, he too would not have hesitated for a moment to consult even Hekate, the dark goddess herself, to save his beloved. In short, he understood. Which did not mean that he, as the camp commander of Vindobona, could simply overlook the accusations against Luscinia, which were probably circulating throughout the city by now.

"And this villa here," he asked with a brisk hand gesture toward the gate, "what brings you here? I heard the master of the house and a slave died recently ... under strange circumstances? Poisoned, rumor has it?"

He fixed his gaze on Layla. He already seemed to suspect why we were here, that it was precisely those deaths that had attracted us, like sweet honey attracts bees.

Layla admitted to him that we were "helping the deceased's spouse cope with the loss," as she put it.

Euphemistic words—which did not deceive Marcellus. He knew Layla's passion for being a snoop well enough.

She didn't mention a word about the baker and her dead son, or even about the fact that Dexippa had hired Layla as an investigator. After all, Marcellus's good nature should not be strained.

"It is the gods themselves who keep leading us to the dead," I said, "or rather, to the murdered! That is not our fault. Nor do we do anything shameful. We are helping the bereaved to solve the death of the *paterfamilias* ... and to avenge it! And Latobios was a highly respected citizen of the city. Surely it is also in your mind that his death should not go unpunished."

"You do realize that you are endangering my reputation with your thoughtless actions," the legate replied. His tone was stern, but he reminded me of a father who had to scold his children but at the same time was glad to have them around again, no matter what mischief they might have pulled, because he loved them with all his heart. Even in his anger, I felt this in Marcellus.

A crazy comparison that had come to my mind, especially considering that Marcellus was young enough to be *my* son.

But, well, our relationship was just something very special. And complicated!

"As for the witch," Marcellus said, "I can't just stand by and watch her do these things, I hope you realize that. I have already sent soldiers to the forest where her camp is said to be. I must first have her arrested. If she is not guilty of any bloodshed, I will let her go unharmed, but I cannot tolerate her activities in my city, no matter how well-meaning they may be. I hope you both understand that. The talk would never end."

"You can't have Luscinia arrested!" I protested. "Not now. Alma is in her custody, in the midst of a dangerous ritual that must not be disturbed."

Marcellus contorted his face. "So let us ride into this witch's camp ourselves. No harm shall come to Alma, on that I give you my word."

He turned to Layla. "You take the car home in the meantime, okay? I'll talk to you later."

He still had a stern expression on his face, but the fleeting smile that flitted across his lips gave him away.

I'll talk to you later, did not mean that he would give her a telling off as soon as he returned home. Quite the opposite....

Even before Layla opened her mouth to answer her lover, I knew she wasn't going home. I could also read her face quite well by now.

"Let me come with you, Marcellus, to the witch's camp. We must look for Alma, if Luscinia will not reveal her whereabouts—and if we have succeeded, she will need a friend by her side."

Marcellus made some counter-argument that I didn't

manage to catch, because I was looking around for my coachman.

I spotted the fellow and my carriage behind the soldiers who were milling about in the forecourt. I gave him a sign that we wanted to get in.

And lo and behold, no sooner had he driven up than Layla breathed a kiss on her legate's cheek, only to climb into the car the very next moment.

"I’m ready," she told me with her famous sphinx’s smile. "Are we going?"

XXIV

Marcellus ordered some of his soldiers to stay behind at Latobios's estate. Apparently he intended to personally attend to solving the murders in the house later. The remaining men followed him on the way into the forest.

Halfway to the witch's camp, we were met by a mounted messenger who belonged to Marcellus's legion. Since my friend rode right next to my wagon, I heard what the man had to tell him.

"We have found the witch's camp, Legate," he cried breathlessly. "We were able to pick up one of the sorceress's assistants, a certain Sagana. And we have searched the camp and already recovered all the witch's implements and supplies."

"And the woman herself?" asked Marcellus.

The messenger bowed his head. "She escaped us, Legate," he mumbled guiltily. "She used a dark spell to deceive our men. She conjured up a mist that hid her ... and then she fled, and we could find no trace of her. She must have turned into an eagle, Legate. Or a wolf, that slipped away on silent paws—"

"Enough of this nonsense," Marcellus interposed. He ordered the legionary to join us, and was already about to set his own horse in motion again.

I addressed him before he could gallop away. "That Luscinia was able to escape while Sagana was apprehended is possibly the will of the gods," I said. "For all we know by now, the witch herself may be innocent, while her assistant was the one casting the bloodthirsty curses, and trying to harm people ... and perhaps even committing two murders."

He didn't reply, just nodded curtly. Marcellus obviously didn't like the fact that someone had escaped from him, regardless of whether the person was guilty or innocent.

He clicked his tongue, spurred his horse, and sat at the head of our procession.

However, before the soldier who had delivered the message from the witch's camp could disappear among his comrades, I called him to me. "Tell me," I asked him with concern, "did you find a young blonde woman in the camp? My Alma...."

The soldier seemed to understand immediately who I was talking about. I did not know him, but he probably was well aware of who I was and apparently even knew Alma, at least by sight. Which was not surprising, after all, as my beloved and I were very often guests of Marcellus in the legionary camp, and the soldiers were always curious about which friends their commander surrounded himself with.

"I'm sorry," the legionary addressed me, "but there was only the assistant after the witch escaped us. She was gathering some belongings, some herbal supplies from one of the tents, when we surprised her. Surely she would have escaped us, too, if we had shown up only a short time later."

"I thank you," I said to the man, then let him go. He joined a group of mounted legionaries who were bringing up the rear of our troop.

Marcellus gave the order to accelerate our travel speed. Soon we were dashing through the forest like a wild-eyed wolf pack. Layla and I were tossed around in my wagon like two sacks of grain and had to make every effort to keep ourselves on the benches.

By the time we reached the camp, it had already been surrounded by Marcellus's soldiers.

I helped Layla out of the car, ignoring the pain in my limbs. It felt like I had just been beaten up. Every bone in my body had been jolted during the wild ride.

Marcellus jumped off his imposing, fiery red stallion a few steps beside us.

I hurried over to him, and Layla followed me. He looked at her first, then let his eyes wander around the camp. Since there was a legionary at every corner, he probably concluded that there was no danger to Layla, and he did not even try to leave her in the wagon.

A higher ranked legionary came rushing toward us. There was nothing good to be read in his face.

"I'm sorry, Legate," he began without mincing his words, but I bring bad news. The assistant of the witch, this Sagana...."

"Yes, what's wrong with her?" Marcellus snapped at the man. He already seemed to suspect that he was about to hear something he wouldn't like one bit.

And so it was. "I'm afraid she managed to escape us as well, Legate," the officer admitted sheepishly. "The two men guarding her swear that she simply vanished into thin air—a spell against which they were powerless, Legate."

Marcellus bared his teeth, but refrained from any comment.

He only sucked in his breath audibly. The way he looked, he would have liked to make the man a head shorter.

But he controlled himself; which did not mean that there would be no repercussions for the legionaries responsible later. Marcellus was a just, but also very strict, commander.

What had happened? With all the dark powers that I believed Sagana to have, I could not seriously imagine that she had actually disappeared into thin air. Presumably she had bewitched, wheedled, and seduced the two legionaries, beguiled their senses ... and then exploited the very moment when the men had been inattentive.

"Find this woman!" Marcellus ordered the officer who had reported to him. He did not shout; on the contrary he spoke very quietly and apparently composedly. "And then bring her to me at once. Understand? I will not tolerate any further failures, you bunglers!"

"As you command, Legate!" Groveling, the man hurried off—visibly relieved that his head was still on his shoulders.

I spoke up. "We have to look for Alma! She won't be in the camp, but somewhere nearby. Maybe in a cave that is supposed to exist here, although I can't say where exactly."

While I was saying these words, full of hope that I would soon be reunited with my beloved, a dark thought entered my mind at the same time as well.

What if Luscinia had taken Alma? Maybe she had kidnapped her or hidden her so well that we would never find her, to have leverage in case the witch was caught during her escape—a free pass for herself in exchange for Alma's life.

"Don't worry, my friend, we'll find her," Marcellus assured me.

He beckoned another of his officers and ordered him to scour the area around the camp with the majority of the available men.

Marcellus himself joined the search, and Layla made a point of following him. I hurried after the two of them, and began to call Alma's name loudly even though I couldn't really hope that she would be able to hear me.

Where had the witch hidden her? My heart contracted as I stumbled over roots and stones, and soon lost all orientation in the forest.

Fortunately, Marcellus was still in sight on my left, together with Layla, who kept up with him nimbly. To my right, I could see and hear a handful of legionaries systematically working their way between the trees.

The cave we knew to exist nearby did not hide from us for too long. We found it at the foot of a densely wooded hill, and immediately set out into its depths. Fortunately, some of the legionaries were equipped with torches and were able to light our way, at least partially.

At this time, at least, we were able to get Layla to wait outside the cave. Marcellus was typically very yielding to her, but if he thought she was in any real danger, there was no arguing with him. She knew that too, and so for once she complied. He and I, as well as some of the legionaries, plunged into the darkness of the cave.

An entrance to the Underworld, went through my head. Luscinia had spoken of this when it came to finding the right place for Alma's healing.

If one could descend through this cave into the realm of the god of the dead, one had to be prepared to encounter creatures on the way that were at home down there, and which had never dared to penetrate to the bright light of day. In the eternal darkness of the cave, only insufficiently illuminated by our torches, they could be dangerous if not deadly opponents.

The cave had seemed small—from the outside—but it soon branched out into several more grottoes and passages. Some of them were so low, or so narrow, that a grown man could barely fit through.

We split up, even though I was reluctant to risk doing so. It was the only way we had a chance to explore the huge labyrinth that opened up before us.

And we achieved a quick success! I had hardly started on my own way when the call of one of the legionaries rang out: "There's someone here! Come quickly!"

I hurried back, running so fast that my torch almost went out—and then I was disappointed. We had indeed discovered a person, and it was not Alma, but Martianus.

He lay with his arms and legs bound in a small but dry and not very drafty cavern. He was also gagged, and I expected that as soon as the men freed him he would hurl wild curses against Luscinia and Avernus, to whom he owed his captivity.

But he did nothing of the sort. He seemed calm and collected, thanked the comrades who had freed him, and greeted the legate when he saw him.

Marcellus instructed a legionary to take him outside, and tend to him there. Martianus appeared unharmed, and did not even seem particularly thirsty or even hungry.

Apparently, Luscinia had taken good care of him until she escaped, even though he was her prisoner.

"We'll talk later." Marcellus bade farewell to the centurion with these terse words, and immediately we continued our search for Alma.

Again we took different paths, and soon I had the feeling of wandering around in this subterranean world all alone and abandoned by all good spirits.

I was careful not to let my torch go out, because I didn't dare imagine how I would find my way down here without any light.

XXV

I called Alma's name, over and over again, moving through caves that seemed to have no end.

Deeper and deeper I worked my way into the bowels of the earth, and soon I was certain that I must have long since crossed the borders of Hades. Strange sounds pursued me, shadows flitted past the walls—which seemed to me like hideous demons—and a smell of mold and decay was in the air.

When I had given up all hope of ever seeing Alma again, she suddenly lay before me. She appeared in the light of my torch like an apparition from the spirit realm: in a small, dry grotto, reminiscent of a vault, she was resting on soft blankets and pillows. Beside her were jars and bowls, an incense burner, and a tiny oil lamp that barely gave any light. A large circle of strange symbols had been painted on the rocky floor around her camp, no doubt the work of Luscinia. Was it a protective circle to keep Alma safe from all evil down here in the bowels of the earth?

Alma was in a deep sleep. I had some trouble waking her up, although I did rush up to her with a wild, happy cry of relief, enfolding her in my arms and covering her face with stormy kisses.

She woke like a sleepy cat, blinked at me from narrow eyes, finally recognized me ... and returned my kisses, even though she was much gentler than I in doing so.

"Dearest, are you all right?" I cried with concern.

Her skin felt warm, thankfully. She wasn't freezing, but she was so skinny and haggard that I could feel her bones when I pressed her against me.

"Nothing can happen to you now, you are safe," I whispered.

She gently detached herself from me, gazing into my eyes in the fitful light of my torch, which I had placed on a ledge.

"I slept," she said then, as if reporting a miracle to me. "Slept for a very long time. Even though Luscinia was with me only a short time ago, a few hours, I think. Or has it been longer than that? It's hard to tell time down here. Hours feel like days, days like weeks.... How long have I been here, Thanar?"

"A few days, dear," I said.

Only then did it dawn on me what I had just heard. "*You slept,*" I repeated as if in a trance, "and didn't dream anything horrible?"

She looked at me, her eyes seeming larger than usual, and her gaze more penetrating, as if she had learned here in the darkness of this Underworld to look right into my soul.

"I dreamed terrible things ... at the beginning," she said after a little while, "worse even than at home. Luscinia was rarely with me in those first hours and days after she led me here. When she came, she spoke magic formulas that I didn't understand, burned fire sacrifices—all to purify and prepare me, she said."

Alma pointed with her hand to a charred little hollow, surrounded by loose stones, in which some ashes lay.

Only now did I notice that a spicy, not unpleasant smell hung in the air, probably emanating from the charred remains. I guessed herbs of some sort, although on closer inspection there were also small parts in the ash that had probably once belonged to beetles or other insects.

"Also, Luscinia brought me potions several times," Alma continued dreamily, "which opened my eyes to the realm of the dead. It's everywhere here, Thanar. All around us."

As if to emphasize her words, she looked around the grotto and seemed to perceive things that were invisible to me.

Quietly and thoughtfully she continued: "Then—I think it was after two or three days, but I can't really say, Luscinia poured me an even stronger potion. I became hot and cold, I suffered pain, I saw terrible demons ... I thought I was going to die. I can hardly remember what she did after that. I think she performed a ritual in which she expelled my tormentors, and then ... I don't remember. I fell into a deep sleep. A dreamless sleep, my love! Can you believe it?"

"Then you are ... healed?" I exclaimed in disbelief.

I kissed her passionately, while she murmured, "I think so, yes, I think I am."

"But where is Luscinia?" she asked me then. "Why are you here? Did she send you?"

"That ... is a longer story, dear. For now, let's get you home, shall we? Then I'll tell you everything in peace. There's been, um, *so* much going on while you've been down here."

Once again, I pressed her against me. Could it really be possible? Had Luscinia done what she had promised us, and actually cured Alma? Did this witch really have the incredible powers that she was said to have had the whole time? Could my Alma have been freed from her tormentors in this dark grotto, where under normal circumstances one would have been more likely to lose one's mind?

Well, the next days would show how things really stood

with her. I didn't dare to hope with all my heart ... but I remembered that now it was necessary to find the way back to the world of the living. And that would not be an easy task.

I can't tell you how long we wandered through the cave before my shouts were finally heard by the legionaries.

I supported Alma while she walked, carried her a bit whenever her strength left her, and once she even fell asleep in my arms while doing so. She had a lot of sleep to catch up on, and my heart beat with joy to see her breathing so calmly and peacefully.

It was a legionary who finally heard my shouts, found his way to us, and showed us the way out.

I carried Alma—with his help—back to the witch's camp, bedded her in my wagon there, and waited quite impatiently until the other members of our search party had also learned that they could stop their efforts. As soon as we had all gathered again, I wanted to get Alma home.

Marcellus and Layla showed up, dirty and tired, yet with bright smiles for Alma's and my sakes.

Layla climbed into the car with Alma, and the two women immediately began a familiar, whispered conversation while holding hands.

I sank down on a stone near the camp's fireplace and breathed freely for the first time.

It was done: Alma was safe, and it even looked like she had actually been healed. I could have screamed with happiness. And I could have sunk into a deep sleep on the spot, too, because I was so exhausted from searching the cave that I could hardly sit upright.

Marcellus joined me, settled down next to me, and kept me company silently, just as a friend, no longer the stern Roman commander.

However, I was not granted too long a reprieve. Twice in quick succession, legionaries came rushing toward us, bringing us news.

The first time, they were dragging two unfortunate fellows to our feet, whom I immediately recognized to be my slaves. They were the men I had sent to the witch's camp in place of Telephus and the wounded Nonius to spy on her.

I quickly vouched for them, and assured Marcellus that they belonged to me and were not prowlers, or even helpers of the witch.

The two confessed the following to me: "We fled, master, when suddenly legionaries appeared in the forest, surrounded the camp and stormed it. We didn't know what the soldiers wanted, so we preferred to leave. We were going to return home, and report to you, Thanar. But then we were caught."

Neither of them knew anything about the escape of Luscinia or Sagana.

"When we fled from the approaching soldiers," said the older of the two, "Sagana was still in the camp. Luscinia had been gone for a while. But she had also disappeared from time to time before. We assumed that she was on her way to gather herbs, or perhaps to check on Martianus or Alma. We didn't follow her on those occasions, but kept an eye on the camp."

"You have acted correctly," I said to the two men, and then I asked Marcellus to release them—which he did. I sent the slaves back to my house. Their spy services here in the forest were no longer necessary.

XXVI

Just as I was about to leave and return to Vindobona, or rather to my house, the arrival of another horseman was announced.

"His name is Telephus," said the legionary who reported to Marcellus, "and he wishes to speak to Thanar. Shall I let him come forward?" He addressed the question to the legate, but at the same time looked at me.

I nodded. "If it's all right with you, Marcellus," I said to my friend. "Perhaps he brings important news."

Telephus was led to us—and had a success to report.

"The boy Timor has been apprehended, Thanar. Today I met with the two men you sent to track him down. I was traveling in the city, looking for Sagana."

"Well, you can stop that search," Marcellus interposed. "She escaped, and is probably long gone, it would seem to me." He sounded ill-tempered, visibly frustrated that the witch's helpmate had escaped his men.

Telephus raised his eyebrows in surprise—and looked guilty. He glanced at me, opened his mouth, and probably wanted to apologize.

But I waved him off. "You're really not to blame for this, my good man."

And turning to the legate, I added, "Your legionaries will find her, Marcellus. And perhaps this time, they won't let themselves be bewitched by her again."

I smiled, but the legate did not reciprocate. He did not like to laugh at the incompetence of his men.

So I turned back to Telephus. "Let's hear what the boy Timor has to say, then," I urged him. "Did you bring him here?" I glanced over his shoulder, but could not spy the lanky figure of the boy anywhere.

"No, I first took him from the two men who had tracked him down—and sent them to your house to report to you, if you were staying there. But I, on the other hand, rode with the boy to the house of Latobios, where I actually suspected you to be. There I was intercepted in the forecourt by the legionaries."

He glanced at Marcellus. "From them, in turn, I learned that you were on your way together to the witch's camp. So I left the boy in the care of the soldiers for later questioning, and rode after you by the quickest route."

Layla let herself be heard from the wagon, which was only a few steps away from us, and where she still sat with Alma: "If it is all right with you, Thanar, Marcellus and I will return with Telephus to the house of Latobios and question Timor, while you take Alma home." She brushed a strand of blond hair from her friend's forehead and gave her an affectionate smile.

Alma, who had been resting with her eyes half-closed, but who nevertheless seemed to have been following every word of our conversation, straightened up.

"No," she contradicted Layla, to my astonishment. "I can find my own way home. Or rather, our coachman will get me there safely, won't he?"

She gave our driver a look in which there was no question, just a friendly smile. And the man also immediately agreed. "Of course, mistress. By the fastest way!"

"There you see, dearest,"—she addressed me—"you don't have to worry about me. So go with Marcellus and Layla, and catch the murderer you're chasing! You already know who he is?"

None of us gave an answer to this question, so Alma continued, "Well, I'm sure you'll expose him!"

I protested, wanting to stay by her and accompany her home, but she just waved me off with a smile.

So it boiled down to Marcellus instructing two legionaries to escort Alma and my carriage safely to my villa, while we made our way to Latobios's estate. To be more precise, we used the car together at first—Alma, Layla and I drove up to Latobios's house, and my coachman and the legionaries then took Alma home. Otherwise, Layla would have had to walk out of the forest.

To let her ride on a horse—even Marcellus was not of such a modern spirit. Although I secretly would not have been surprised if our black sphinx had mounted a steed in front of our very eyes.

To my astonishment, the legate did not reproach Layla again over the fact that she had been investigating murders behind his back. And I have to admit that I was eager to work with her to solve our latest, most perplexing case.

I wondered what the boy Timor would have to say. Would he talk—and reveal something that could expose the murderer? In the end, would we be able to convict Smertius as a patricide?

XXVII

Telephus, who had followed us on horseback, was the first to jump out of the saddle in the forecourt of Latobios's estate. He turned to one of the legionaries who were standing guard there, but I did not hear what he said. It was only a few words.

The legionary nodded, then disappeared at a run into one of the outbuildings. Immediately after, he and a second soldier dragged the boy Timor into the square. The boy resisted the rough treatment, shouting loudly several times, "Leave me alone! I have done nothing; I am innocent!"

Telephus received the boy, bent over him—he was a good head taller—and seemed to talk to him soothingly.

Anyway, the boy gave up his resistance, and finally we all entered the villa together. In the atrium, Smertius met us, his eyes widening in terror at the sight of Marcellus and the handful of soldiers who had entered the house in his wake.

"What has ... happened?" asked Smertius uncertainly.

His gaze fell on Timor. "Why did you bring him back? Is he—my father's murderer?"

Marcellus ordered the majority of his men to withdraw from the villa with a curt wave of his hand. Only two of the legionaries remained with us, but kept discreetly in the background.

"No need to worry you," the legate said to Smertius, as I walked up to the youth and raised my hands placatingly.

"Timor is merely to be interrogated," I explained, "and we

would also like to speak to you and your mother again, in the presence of the legate."

I cast a sidelong glance at Marcellus. Referring to him never failed to have an effect on people. Wealthy men like Smertius might not fear him, but he always inspired great respect in them, too.

Smertius sent two of his slaves to provide us with refreshments, then he escorted us to one of his arcaded courtyards, and had us sit down on a group of comfortable couches and chairs in the shade of the rounded arches. He sent another slave to fetch Hersilia, and the lady of the house appeared shortly thereafter, accompanied by her body servant.

Today she looked dejected as usual, and did not seem eager to receive guests, but wrung a few polite words out of herself. Then she settled down on the bench next to Layla.

Marcellus said, "As I have heard, there is a need to solve the murder of the master of the house—and rest assured that we will expose the culprit."

With that, he gave me the floor. After all, he was not actually familiar with the details of the case itself.

"The death of the master of the house," I confirmed, "and of his scribe, Chelion."

I turned to the boy Timor.

"You left this house shortly after Chelion was murdered. And only a little later, Latobios was found dead."

The boy opened his eyes in fright.

"I ... had nothing to do with it! I bought myself free, sir," he stammered. "It was all in order! I paid the master the price he demanded, and he released me." He turned to Hersilia with a helpless look.

She sat there limp and paralyzed, but the boy's words shook her up a little.

She straightened her back, even though it seemed to cost her an infinite amount of strength. Then she cleared her throat, as if she first had to find her voice again.

Finally she nodded, and said, "Timor speaks the truth. I was there when my husband released him into freedom, and he has not returned since then—that would have been noticed in this house. So he is completely innocent of my husband's fate! I'm sure he wasn't even around."

Layla took over proceedings, and turned to the boy herself.

"Why did you want to leave?" she asked Timor. "What aroused in you the desire to gain your freedom at this very particular time? Surely you had the necessary sum together for some time?"

"Not so fast," Marcellus interjected. "I think it's rather strange that such a young fellow as you has already saved up so much. I'd be interested to know how you got the money in the first place."

Turning to me, he added, "That detail does seem significant, don't you think, Thanar?"

I nodded in agreement and stifled a smile. The whole case, and even this interrogation, did not fall under Marcellus's jurisdiction as legate of Vindobona. But he also loved—at least secretly—to act as a puzzle solver, and a murder investigator.

"I saved up the money!" exclaimed Timor. "Every single sesterce. From the tips the master and mistress gave me—I am not a thief!"

"Nobody's saying that," I interjected again.

Before Marcellus could unsettle the boy further, I quickly added, "What was it, then, that connected you with Chelion? You were often seen in his presence. And he was also observed giving you money, and you receiving it."

The latter was a lie, a true shot in the dark, but there were not too many possibilities regarding how Timor could have gotten the money for his ransom. He really couldn't have already saved it up at such a young age, even if he did insist on it. Only a master's very favorite slave could have received such lavish tips.

So in the end there were only two possibilities: first, that he had stolen the money after all. Or second, that he'd received special favors from someone else. If Chelion had really been his lover, he might have paid Timor for his affection.

Chelion certainly had had more money than the boy, and definitely could have gotten more from his mother if he'd had a need for it. Which reminded me, however, of the still unanswered question of why *he* by comparison had not ransomed himself.

"That's not true," the boy cried fervently. "I never took money from Chelion. And he and I were merely friends, nothing more."

Why was it so important to the boy to deny his relationship with the murdered scribe, I asked myself, and not for the first time. After all, it was not a capital crime to become closer friends with one of the other slaves, and most masters had little objection to love affairs among the servants. After all, relationships between men and women could produce children, i.e. inexpensive slave offspring for the house. And if two men enjoyed themselves with each other, there was no real disadvantage to their owner.

So why was Timor so insistent that nothing had happened between him and Chelion? I was sure that the boy was hiding something from us, that he was lying. But *why*?

"I don't think it was Chelion who gave Timor the money for the ransom," Layla suddenly interrupted us.

She looked first at me, then at Marcellus. In her eyes was once again that expression that reminded me of a hound on a hot trail.

"That wouldn't make sense, I don't think," she continued. "Because if Timor really was Chelion's lover—and Chelion himself couldn't buy himself free—why would he have helped his lover get out of the house?"

"He was not my lover!" cried the boy imploringly. "Please believe me!"

"I believe you," Layla said, "I really do. But tell me, Timor, speaking of ransoming: why hadn't Chelion actually bought his own freedom already? His mother is not a poor woman—"

"I ... I really don't know," the boy stammered.

Layla continued: "Latobios assured us that he would not have denied freedom to any of his slaves if they could raise the necessary sum. And I didn't get the impression that he was so attached to his scribe that he couldn't spare him. Therefore I think there is only one possible explanation as to why Chelion did not leave the house—he *wanted to* stay."

Timor said nothing in reply, but I saw him nervously intertwine his slender fingers, knead them, and then disengage them. Layla was on the trail of something that was worrying the boy. But what was she getting at?

She didn't keep us guessing for long, because she immediately continued, "Chelion wanted to stay here for the one reason that you'd endure everything. Captivity, slavery, servitude ... for love, I think. But not for you Timor, am I not right?"

The boy swallowed, but did not answer.

"But to whom did his heart belong, that he remained a slave for the sake of this person? If it had been someone else among the servants, man or woman, Chelion would not have had to keep it a secret."

Layla turned her gaze to Smertius. "And if he had been your lover, or your father's, he would not have had to make a secret of it either. It is, after all, common for a master to keep a favorite slave. Be it a man or a woman."

Was it just my imagination, or did Layla turn her head in my direction for a brief moment at these words? She, who had once been my slave, whom I had loved so very much....

She didn't give me time to think about it, because she continued—by now quite fired up—"There was only one person in this house that Chelion wasn't allowed to love."

XXVIII

Now, Layla clearly turned her head, but not in my direction. "Isn't that so ... Hersilia?" She looked squarely at the lady of the house, not unkindly, but still very determinedly.

Hersilia's mouth opened, but no sound passed her lips. Suddenly color shot into her ivory-white cheeks. "I..." she began.

"*You* gave Timor the money to buy his freedom, didn't you, Hersilia?" said Layla. "When Chelion was dead, you no longer needed the boy's services. For Timor was your confidant, I think, your messenger, your alibi ... the one here in the house who helped you keep your relationship a secret. And after you lost Chelion, and we started asking Timor questions about him, you thought it wise to get the boy out of the house so that he might not disclose anything that would reveal the truth to us."

Smertius jumped up indignantly.

"Is that true, Mother?" he snapped at Hersilia. "Did you cheat on my father, with this ... this...."

He couldn't find the right words, just gasped and stared angrily at Hersilia.

Finally, he dropped back into his seat and uttered a soft curse. "My mother is a whore," I heard him mutter.

And Hersilia did not miss these words of abuse. "Call me what you will, miscreant!" she hurled at her son in a burst of sudden anger.

She raised her head and let her eyes wander around the

room, all at once as proud as a queen. Then she addressed Layla.

"It is true what you say; I won't deny it any longer, because what else have I got to lose? The dearest thing in the world was taken from me. Chelion—he was my everything, my light, my life. And he felt the same for me!"

Smertius uttered another angry sound, and contorted his face as if he had bitten into a rotten fruit. His hands clenched into fists.

Timor stood there like a pillar of salt. His cheeks glowed red, and his gaze was fixed on Hersilia, whom he really had served faithfully.

I had the suspicion that this seemingly tender boy would have kept silent unto death, that he would not have revealed the secret of his mistress at any price. He had well earned his freedom for his loyalty, I thought.

Hersilia began to recount her story. "For Latobios, I was nothing more than an ornament. His love was only ever for his horses. I was only a piece of jewelry, which he acquired in order to be able to present a pretty wife in the company of others. He called me beautiful, found me attractive, I believe that—but he never loved me. He just wanted to possess me, and my father practically sold me to him. He was a highly respected man, my father, but in dire financial straits. And Latobios, the rising star among the charioteers at that time, offered him a handsome sum for me. So much gold that father could not resist. I thought then that my life was over, and that I would never be happy again."

"Until Chelion came into your house," Layla said.

Hersilia nodded. A fleeting smile flashed across her lips.

"Latobios bought him from a friend in Vindobona, who already owned Chelion's mother. To me he was a gift from the gods. We knew after only a few months that we were meant for each other, and we tried to escape. That is, I stole away in the middle of the night. Chelion was not to follow me until I had actually succeeded in absconding. I left him money, so that he could buy himself free after some time inconspicuously, in order to then travel after me. I wanted it that way, because I would never have endangered his life. I said to myself, if Latobios catches me, he will hardly kill me. After all, I am his wife. But Chelion, if he escapes with me, if it came out that I love him...."

She shook her head. "Latobios would have beaten him to death—and gotten away with it. After all, he was only a slave."

"Your escape failed, I take it?" said Layla.

Hersilia lowered her head into her hands. "It did. Chelion and I, we wanted to start a new life, in a distant province, somewhere in the west where no one knew us. But I didn't even get two days into my journey."

She reached for Layla's hand, as if she had to hold on somewhere to be able to bear the memories she conjured up. "Fortuna failed me," she said. "Latobios was not willing to let me go. He saw only the disgrace I would have caused him had I successfully escaped from my husband. He sent half an army of henchmen after me ... and I did not succeed in escaping them."

She raised her head and looked at Smertius, who had turned away in disgust.

"I was right in thinking that Latobios would not kill me if my plan failed," she continued. "He let me live ... but only by a hair's breadth. He beat me half to death, and not only once—and with this punishment, without knowing it, extinguished another life—that of an unborn child. You see, I was expecting when I fled, if you must know."

She looked at Layla as if she wanted to reveal the whole truth to her, as if she were speaking confidentially with a friend who would understand her.

Layla squeezed Hersilia's hand, which was still holding hers. "Was Chelion the father of this child?" she asked.

"Oh, certainly, for Latobios hardly ever touched me. As I said, for him I was just a pretty ornament. He was neither interested in me, nor in a family, apart from the fact that he had to produce a successor at some point, an heir to his name and fortune. You were conceived six months later, Smertius," she said, addressing her son. "But you were never a substitute for that child I lost. The one I had conceived in true love."

"You have never been a good mother to me," the youth hurled at her. "And now I know why. I was the child of the man you hated! And even though I didn't understand then why you rejected me, I felt it, every day of my life! Get out of my sight, you disgust me. This is no longer your house!"

He jumped up and was about to storm off, but Marcellus also got to his feet and stepped in his way. "Stay here. We're not done yet," he said in a firm voice, ordering the young man back to his seat.

"Are you going to tell me what to do, Legate? In my own house?" Smertius roared.

"That's exactly what I am doing," Marcellus returned unapologetically. "Now sit down!"

The young man obeyed. He may have been the proud new

master of the house, but he was still a boy at heart—and I almost felt sorry for him now. His father had only been interested in horses, his mother had never wanted him ... truly not a nice fate for a growing child.

Smertius dropped back onto his couch in the shade of the archway and avoided looking Marcellus in the eye.

A thought popped into my head—more precisely, I realized the significance of an observation I had just made. For Smertius had been most indignant when Hersilia had confessed her love for Chelion, but he had not really seemed surprised.

"You already knew, didn't you?" I began, fixing my gaze firmly on Smertius. "That your mother was having an affair with Chelion."

He raised his head and waved my words aside with a condescending hand gesture. But it didn't seem worth his while to actually contradict me.

"I don't know how you found out, but in the end that doesn't matter," I continued. "What matters is that you begrudged the mother who couldn't love you her happiness. You were disgusted that she slept with a slave. You wanted to take revenge, to punish her, didn't you? Maybe even defend your father's honor, so that he would finally realize he could be proud of you. You killed Chelion!"

XXIX

"That makes sense," Marcellus cut in, "when you consider how Chelion died. If Latobios himself had gotten wise to his wife and her lover, he wouldn't have had to poison his own slave in secret. He would have executed him, I should think. I knew Latobios only slightly, but he was a proud and sometimes quite irascible man."

"And no one else in the house had any reason to kill Chelion," I said. "He was well-liked, and friendly. An affable person."

Smertius sat there with a petrified expression on his face, and did not speak a word. But he did not deny my accusations either.

I continued to explore my theme. "So you knew about Chelion and your mother. And you wanted to act ... but you may not have had a plan at first as to exactly how to proceed. Then, as if by a happy twist of fate, Luscinia came to the house to heal the sick horse, and in her wake came Sagana—an attractive young woman who caught your eye. She was merely the witch's assistant, but already well versed in the arts of magic herself. And unlike Luscinia, she was willing to work dark magic ... as long as the price was right. She thirsted for gold, for power, for social advancement. And the son of a millionaire, in whom she saw an easy mark, probably came just in time for her."

"She saw what was in me," Smertius protested, "and yes, I liked her. It's my business who I give my favors to!"

"She wanted to steal her mistress's spell book," I said, "even though it may not even have existed—and you helped her, didn't you? You were being watched, my boy! Sagana kept the witch busy in the camp while you searched the nearby cave that Luscinia used for her rituals for a possible secret hiding place. Is that where Sagana suspected the book to be?"

Smertius did not give me an answer.

"Well, either way," I said, "I don't care what you've been up to with Sagana, what plans you pursued. I only maintain that she procured for you the necessary poison to kill Chelion, and that's exactly what you did. To get back at the mother who didn't want you."

These words seemed to stir something in Smertius.

He jerked his head up, jutting his chin out.

"That's right!" he suddenly cried. "I don't deny it, and she deserved it, this whore who calls herself my mother! They both deserved it—Chelion, who cuckolded my father, and that harlot who threw herself into the arms of a slave!"

He straightened his shoulders and stared at us defiantly. "What are you going to do about it? Arrest me for killing a slave? He was my father's property, whose heir I now am. And Father would hardly have charged me for destroying his property. He could buy ten new slaves—even a hundred, if he had felt like it."

His voice swelled. "On the contrary, he would have been grateful to me for judging and executing the faithless slave who so disgustingly betrayed him. Chelion deserved to die—and Father might have seen at last what I was made of. I had every intention of revealing the truth to him! About Chelion, and my mother! Before he died, too."

"You are right,"—Marcellus took the floor—"we can't prosecute you for the dead slave. But as a patricide, we most certainly can. Had you acquired a taste for handling the witches' poisons? Did Sagana whisper to you that it would be a good opportunity to free yourself from the tyrant who didn't take you seriously, who didn't even see you? Because he was so enamored with his noble horses?"

"What? No!" protested Smertius. "I would never have done anything to my father! He might not have thought much of me, because I would never grow up to be a victorious racer like he was, yet I adored him. I only ever treated him with the proper respect of a good son!"

Marcellus continued unmoved: "Finally having the say here in the house yourself. And then to disown your hated mother, as you hinted at earlier ... the temptation must have been great."

"And Sagana helped you again," I intervened.

I was sure that Marcellus was right in his accusation. Why hadn't I thought of it myself?

Quickly I continued, "Sagana saw the chance to conquer you completely and take you for herself. As soon as your father was no longer alive, she could perhaps even become your wife, if she only wooed and enchanted you completely with her witch's powers. A young millionaire, a life of luxury ... what a prospect!"

"It wasn't like that!" exclaimed Smertius. "Sagana wasn't after my money. She—she simply found me attractive. Is that so incomprehensible? And I didn't harm a hair on my father's head!"

A tortured sound escaped Hersilia. She sank stunned

against Layla's shoulder and fanned herself with her hand.

"I can't believe what you're saying," she moaned. "What did I raise? A snake, nurtured at my own breast!"

Her bosom rose and fell, and she struggled for breath. She seemed to be on the verge of collapse.

The body slave, who was standing behind her bench, leaned forward anxiously.

"Are you not feeling well, mistress? Can I get you something? A glass of herbal wine? Do you want to lie down?" She sounded genuinely concerned.

Hersilia clung to Layla's arm. "I'm all right," she gasped.

Then she ordered the slave, "Just bring me my elixir, please. It will help me to calm down. You will find it in my dressing room, in the little chest with my cosmetics...."

The slave girl scurried away. "I'll be right back, mistress," she called as she ran along the arcade, and immediately disappeared into the main wing of the house.

Hersilia made a visible effort to bring her breathing back under control. She was still clinging to Layla, her eyelids flickering, but she repeated mechanically, "I'm sorry. I'll be all right—I'll be all right—"

But instead of calming down, she fell into a half-mad litany: "My son ... a murderer. Who stole my beloved and poisoned his own father. Oh, shame and disgrace!"

"Be silent!" exclaimed Smertius. "You dare to judge me, you, who fornicated with a slave? I only put an end to your shameful doings. I have not touched my father. I swear by all the gods!"

Hersilia began to howl and clamor. She buried her face in her hands.

Layla tried hard to calm her down, but had little success. I only hoped that the body slave would return soon with the elixir, and that this would quiet the poor mistress of the house.

Hersilia had really been through a lot. I didn't even want to imagine how she must have spent her life. Disregarded and then beaten half to death by her own husband, deprived of a child she would've nurtured, bound in love to a man who was forbidden to her....

After a short while, the body slave finally reappeared. She carried a small blue glass bottle with her, which she immediately unplugged and handed to her mistress.

Hersilia eagerly put it to her lips, to plunge the contents down her throat—but then she suddenly snatched the vial away again, as if she had burned herself on the glass. She let out a new cry, even more pitiful and agonized than before, and held out the elixir to her son.

"Drink, then, woman," Marcellus demanded impatiently.

Hersilia shook her head vigorously. "What if I was the one my son was really trying to kill?" she cried. "The thought just came to me, as I was about to drink!"

She was breathing heavily, but seemed to be back to a somewhat clearer mind. "Because you know, Legate, it really doesn't fit that he wanted to kill his father. He worshipped him with an almost dog-like devotion. And Latobios and I dined together, the day he died, just before he went into the bath and perished there. We didn't do that often; I stayed out of his way as much as possible ... but that day, it did happen. And my husband ate some of my food because I didn't feel any appetite. So I ask you: what if the poisoned dish, the poisoned drink was really meant for me? Am I still safe to take my strengthening potion, which my son knows about and which he may also have meddled with?"

"You truly deserve to die," Smertius hurled hatefully at his mother, "but you can take your stupid potion. Perhaps it will help you not to act like a foolish woman before the legate!"

Now he jumped up, and ran towards her. She jerked back, as if she feared he might try to hit her.

But he merely reached for her hand, snatched the small blue vial from her fingers and took a hearty swig from it. Then he pressed it back into her hand.

"There, you see it! I am not a poisoner! I didn't want to kill you, even if you deserved it. And I would never have killed my father."

He looked around, seeking Marcellus's attention in particular. "Do you believe me now, Legate?"

Marcellus did not speak a word. But Hersilia now seemed to accept Smertius's assertion—and his demonstrative act. She let herself sink back against Layla's shoulder, and drank in greedy gulps from the vial.

Then she closed her eyelids and moaned softly. She seemed to trust that the potion would soon take effect and calm her down.

Marcellus, on the other hand, was unimpressed.

"Great words, young man," he said, turning to Smertius, "but you do not deceive me with your skillful rhetoric. Everything is against you. Let the court decide whether you are guilty or innocent."

He turned to his two soldiers, who had stayed in the background until now. "Put him in fetters and mount him on a horse. We're done here." With these words he rose.

Smertius spouted a new torrent of words to try to convince Marcellus of his innocence.

But the two legionaries jumped forward and grabbed hold of the young man. They dragged him away while Smertius roared and clamored and continued to claim his innocence.

"I think you're acting correctly, Legate," I said to Marcellus. "A few days in the dungeon will loosen his tongue, I think. He had the strongest motive here in the house to kill Latobios. And he had the means and the knowledge of how to use poisons, thanks to Sagana. He's our man—he has to be."

We borrowed one of the estate's cars, so Layla wouldn't have to walk to the legionary camp.

Marcellus and I rode with her instead of mounting our horses. We followed the troop of soldiers who hurried ahead of us, carrying the bound Smertius with them.

I decided to have another cup of wine with my friend at the Legate's Palace and restore peace between us. He would forgive me for what I had done with the witch—whom I had turned to only because of Alma. And I would make it clear to him that Layla was not to blame, neither for our dealings with Luscinia, nor for the fact that we had become involved in another murder case. I didn't want Layla to get into trouble, or for Marcellus to resent her for too long.

Layla sat broodingly next to us in the car and seemed to be deeply lost in thought.

"Aren't you glad that the case is solved?" I asked her. *That you can tell your baker the murderer of her son,* I added in my mind. Marcellus was not to know anything about that job. He would have been terribly upset if he knew that Layla had now put the idea of us being Detectores into practice after all.

"Layla?" I asked, and this time she raised her head and looked at me.

"I think..." she began, but then suddenly the hoofbeats of a galloping horse were heard.

The next moment a single horseman appeared on the road

in front of us, and quickly approached us. I recognized in him one of the legionaries who had ridden ahead with Smertius to the legionary camp.

"Legate!" he shouted when he reached us and, breathing heavily, reined in his horse. "A misfortune has befallen us. The prisoner is dead!"

"What are you saying, man?" Marcellus jumped out of the wagon and rushed toward the legionary. The latter's horse reared reflexively as my friend stood up in front of him.

"I saw it with my own eyes, Legate!" the man shouted as he regained control of the animal.

The legionary heaved himself down from of the saddle, bowed his head to Marcellus, then continued: "Smertius suddenly complained of nausea, Legate. Which, of course, did not impress us. We thought he was trying a feint. He began to groan and breathe heavily, then doubled over. Suddenly he was foaming at the mouth, and right after that he fell out of the saddle. When he hit the road, he was dead, Legate! The men think that the Furies executed him before we could do so. That they carried off the patricide ... it was a gruesome sight, I swear to you."

Marcellus stood there motionless for a moment, then he composed himself. He half turned to me and said, "Well, good, so be it. He could hardly have expected a better fate in our hands. So we'll just save ourselves the trouble of putting him on trial, and surely it is for the best that we do not have to execute the son of one of the richest inhabitants of Vindobona."

Marcellus dismissed the messenger, then climbed back into the carriage with us, and ordered the coachman to drive on.

But Layla intervened. "It wasn't the Furies who judged Smertius, dearest," she cried excitedly. "He was murdered—and I know by whom."

"*Murdered*?" repeated Marcellus incredulously.

"Please let the car turn around," implored Layla. "We have to go back to the house of Latobios. Maybe it's not too late!"

"Too late for what?"

"To arrest the real murderer," cried Layla. "Please, so let us turn!"

Marcellus complied with her request. In his usual commanding tone, he instructed the coachman to turn the carriage around at the next widening of the road. But he seemed to understand just as little of what Layla now had in mind as I did myself.

I will make it short, so as not to plunge the inclined readers of my chronicle into the same confusion that befell my friend and me: when we reached the house of Latobios, it was already indeed too late.

The servants were in an uproar, and we immediately learned that Hersilia had also and quite suddenly breathed her last, just like her son on the way to his captivity. Hersilia had complained of great nausea, then pain, and had collapsed.

And finally Layla explained herself to us: "It was Hersilia who killed Latobios—not Smertius. She also judged her son for taking her lover. She poisoned him in front of all of us. And as I watched. Oh, how blinded I have been!"

"Wait," I cried, "you mean ... the vial? The supposed sedative elixir she had brought to her?"

Layla nodded vigorously. "It was not a tonic, but pure poison. She gave it to her son to avenge Chelion—and then drank from it herself to evade judgment. She had to know that we would understand what she had done as soon as Smertius died in our custody. And I imagine," Layla added more quietly, in an almost melancholic tone, "that she didn't want to live anyway, now that her beloved had been taken from her. That's why she already had the poison at hand; she drank it, not only to elude us, but to follow Chelion into the world of the dead."

I ruffled my hair. Layla's words had hit me as unexpectedly as punches.

"I would never have thought of that idea," I had to admit. "That Hersilia kept poison in that vial and so boldly committed murder with it—in front of all of us."

"We should have realized it sooner!" Layla rebuked us, and especially herself. "There was more than one clue, after all. If Hersilia took the potion as often as she claimed to her son, why did she have to explain to her body slave where the vial would be found?"

"True enough," Marcellus grumbled.

"And another thing," Layla said, "Hersilia herself stated that she lunched with Latobios the day he died, and that it did not happen often. I'm sure she arranged that meal for one purpose only: so that she could poison him."

"But why did she do that?" I objected. "Surely it wasn't he who took her lover from her. Or did she simply want to revenge herself on him for ruining her life before she herself passed away? Did she long for retribution for the unborn child he once took from her?"

A crying slave girl escorted us to Hersilia's chamber, where the lady of the house lay dead on the bed.

"We found this on her," the slave said, handing us an opened wax tablet. It was densely written with small, neat letters.

"A farewell note?" I asked as Marcellus picked up the tablet. Layla and I bent curiously over the text, and the legate began to read aloud.

Chelion, I hasten to you, beloved, began the message. *Never again shall we be separated!*

What followed was a kind of confession, even if it read more like a dry factual report and did not show any hint of remorse.

It was I who poisoned Latobios. I did it because I believed that he had taken Chelion from me. And I had this knowledge from Luscinia; after the death of my beloved, I went to her and implored her to use her clairvoyant powers for me. I asked of her who had killed Chelion. She called upon the gods ... and finally told me that Latobios had done it.

So I planned his death.

But Luscinia was wrong, as I learned today! It was my son who robbed me of my beloved. So now I had to take my revenge on him too, and I have done so. Now I can go in peace!

Farewell!

When Marcellus had finished speaking, we stood there wordlessly. None of us knew what to say to this course of events, to this family drama that would have been worthy of a Greek poet.

"Do you remember, Thanar,"—Layla finally found her voice again—"that Telephus was watching Hersilia visit the witch? That must have been when she questioned Luscinia about her lover's death, about who took Chelion's life. And now I understand why Hersilia behaved so strangely when I first came to see her. She was in deepest grief, in despair because the dearest thing in her world had been taken from her, but she was not allowed to show these feelings to anyone so as not to betray her secret love."

"It seems to me that Luscinia's visit to this house has brought a lot of suffering," I said, "apart from the fact that she was able to cure Latobios's horse. Smertius met Sagana, and became a poisoner, robbing his mother of her lover. And Hersilia herself sought out the witch she had met in her own house—to learn on whom her revenge must be taken."

"And Luscinia was wrong," I said. "She healed the horse, she helped my Alma, it seems, and she may indeed never cast dark spells. But with her clairvoyant scrying for Hersilia, she went wrong in the worst way! And thereby she is complicit in Latobios's death."

"Little did she know what Hersilia would do with the knowledge she revealed to her," Layla said.

The Furies, the goddesses of vengeance, may not have been responsible for Smertius's death, but they did eventually take a victim. Sagana, the witch's fugitive assistant, was also found dead, just a few days later in a wooded area to the west of the city. It appeared she had fallen victim to a pack of wolves.

Luscinia, on the other hand, remained missing—as if she had actually disappeared into thin air.

I suspected that she had moved on to a distant province, and could hopefully build a better reputation for herself there—now without her murderous sidekick—than in Vindobona.

About two weeks after the events of this chronicle, a letter arrived from her. It was addressed to Layla, and it contained the recipe for the eye elixir that the witch had brewed for Telephus.

I think you have the necessary skills to brew new supplies for Telephus, Luscinia wrote. *He will probably have to use the elixir for a long time, to stop the deterioration of his eyesight in the long run. I reveal to you here the recipe, the effectiveness of which lies mainly in the herbs, and does not require any magical powers.*

The postscript of the letter was about Alma:

I trust that you have recovered your friend, and that she is cured of her nightmares.

Layla immediately set to work procuring the listed herbs—

some of which grew in her garden—and making the elixir for Telephus.

Avernus, the medicus, was dismissed from the Legion under the cover of silence.

Marcellus could not tolerate that one of his own doctors had taken a patient—an officer at that—to a witch for healing.

But Avernus was not angry over this judgment. He wanted to look for Luscinia, he told me when I saw him for the last time.

"She is such a remarkable woman," he said, "and an excellent healer. Together we could do great things, I feel. For the sick, the suffering, the possessed...."

As far as Luscinia's healing skills were concerned, I could only agree with him. Alma had not been haunted by any nightmares since that day I had found her in the cave. I could have embraced the witch for that—even if she might truly be a miserable clairvoyant.

Alma's nights—and therefore mine—were no longer filled with cries of fear and sleeplessness. That is, we may have remained sleepless, but for the most beautiful of reasons, which I do not need to explain to the experienced reader here. I will only say that Cupid was kind to us, and we thought of ourselves as his very special favorites.

Layla was able to tell her client Dexippa the name of the man who had killed her son: Smertius. Layla did this secretly, without Marcellus knowing of it. And the baker insisted on paying her a decent fee for her services in return.

Gorgonius reconciled with his wife, who overcame her illness. He swore to me that he would never again doubt her love, and that he would not seek out a witch again in his life, either. At the same time, he begged me not to betray him to Marcellus. He did not want to suffer the same fate as—or a worse one than—Avernus, and become an outcast of the legion.

I complied with his request, but at the same time let him know that I would be keeping an eye on him. If I ever learned again that he was guilty of a violent act, I would reveal everything to Marcellus.

He accepted this condition only too willingly.

And Martianus, the centurion who almost became Avernus's murderer?

He no longer screamed or raved, but instead had lapsed into a deep brooding silence since we had freed him from the cave. Was this now the natural grief of a father for his son—which would eventually be alleviated to the point where he could once again become a full member of the Legion?

I hoped so. For the time being, he was taken to Aquae, south of Vindobona, to the military hospital there. It was a place where severely injured people were cared for, and the doctors also had experience with mental confusion. Now we had to wait and see if they could help Martianus there.

As far as I was concerned, I was looking forward to a few quiet and relaxing days, or even weeks—unaware that a new disaster was already looming on the horizon.

Dramatis personae

Thanar: Germanic merchant with a weakness for Roman lifestyle and culture.
Layla: Thanar's freedwoman and former lover, from the legendary kingdom of Nubia. Passionate sleuth and puzzle solver.

Alma Philonica: Thanar's mistress
Titus Granius Marcellus: Legate (commander) of the legionary camp of Vindobona. Layla's lover.

Telephus: a former gladiator, in Thanar's service
Nemesis: gladiatrix, guest of Thanar
Optimus: veteran of the Legion, guest of Thanar

Luscinia: a witch
Sagana: her helper
Bedran: Luscinia's servant

Latobios: legendary charioteer, son of Vindobona and a millionaire
Hersilia: his wife
Smertius: their son

Chelion: deceased reader and scribe of Latobios
Dexippa: his mother, a baker
Timor: a boy, slave in the house of Latobios
Olivia: a female slave in the house of Latobios

Lucius Avernus: medicus in the camp hospital of Vindobona
Sergius Martianus: centurion in the legionary camp of Vindobona
Gorgonius: optio in the legionary camp of Vindobona

More from Alex Wagner:

If you enjoyed *Cursed to Die*, why not try my contemporary mystery series, too?—*Penny Küfer Investigates*—cozy crime novels full of old world charm.

About the author:

Alex Wagner lives with her husband and 'partner in crime' near Vienna, Austria. From her writing chair she has a view of an old ruined castle, which helps her to dream up the most devious murder plots.
Alex writes historical as well as contemporary murder mysteries, always trying to give you sleepless nights. ;)

You can learn more about the author and her books here:

www.alexwagner.at
www.facebook.com/AlexWagnerMysteryWriter
www.instagram.com/alexwagner_author

Publisher: Alexandra Wagner

Editor: Tarryn Thomas
Cover design: Estella Vukovic

Made in the USA
Las Vegas, NV
01 March 2024